"Come Out With Me Tomorrow Night.

"We'll talk and relax. You need a break, and so do I." Cord knew he was taking a chance. He needed to get Victoria out of his system some way. Maybe if he spent time with her as a woman he could find the friend. It was a long shot and not even completely logical, but he had to try something before he lost her completely.

Victoria froze. She gazed into his eyes, searching his expression. The blandness of it warned her to tread carefully. "Why?"

"Why not? Afraid?"

"Of what?"

"Me?" He got to his feet, watching her back away until she came up against the wall. All the promises he had made to himself about how to come to terms with his desire for her went up in smoke. He couldn't see her without wondering what she would feel like in his arms, responding to him as a man. He should walk away, but even that was beyond him.

"I'm not afraid of any man," Victoria taunted him.

"Good." His head bent to kiss her. He had been denying himself for too long to stop now.

Dear Reader:

Happy Holidays to all of you!

This December brings not only three sensational books by familiar favorites—Jennifer Greene, Annette Broadrick and Sara Chance—but wonderful stories from a couple of newcomers: Jackie Merritt and Terry Lawrence. There's also a fabulous Christmas bonus, *'Tis the Season* by Noreen Brownlie, a novel full of the Christmas spirit about the best gift of all—the gift of love.

January marks the beginning of a very special new year, a twelve-month extravaganza with Silhouette Desire. We've declared 1989 the Year of the Man, and we're spotlighting one book each month as a tribute to the Silhouette Desire hero—our Man of the Month!

Created by your favorite authors, you'll find these men utterly irresistible. You'll be swept away by Diana Palmer's Mr. Janaury, (whom some might remember from a brief appearance in *Fit for a King*), and Joan Hohl's Mr. February is every woman's idea of the perfect Valentine....

Don't let these men get away!

Yours,

Isabel Swift
Senior Editor & Editorial Coordinator

SARA CHANCE
Southern Comfort

Silhouette Desire

Published by Silhouette Books New York

America's Publisher of Contemporary Romance

SILHOUETTE BOOKS
300 East 42nd St., New York, N.Y. 10017

Copyright © 1988 by Sydney Ann Clary

ISBN: 0-373-05467-X

First Silhouette Books printing December 1988

SARA CHANCE

lives on Florida's Gold Coast. With the ocean two minutes from home, a boat in the water in the back-yard and an indoor swimming pool three feet from her word processor, is it any wonder she loves swimming, fishing and boating? Asked why she writes romance, she replies, "I live it and believe in it. After all, I met and married my husband, David, in less than six weeks." That was two teenage daughters and twenty years ago. Two of Sara's Desires, *Her Golden Eyes* and *A Touch of Passion*, were nominated by Romantic Times in the Best Desires category for their publishing years. And *Double Solitaire* was a Romance Writers of America Golden Medallion nominee.

One

Victoria Wynne reached for the roll of plans on the shelf behind her. Her sleek black hair, done in its usual French braid for the office, shone with a rich sheen beneath the artificial light of the drafting table. Sun poured in the floor-to-ceiling windows behind her, casting shadows over fine-boned features and dark sapphire eyes. She was leggy with a willowy figure that any woman would envy. Many had called her beautiful in college, but she had rarely noticed. She had been too busy taking her degree in landscape architecture and, later, too determined to climb to the top of her profession, a goal that had been interrupted with marriage to George Wynne.

The disaster, Cord Darcourte had called it when Victoria's life had taken a new turn and she had become a wife. Victoria didn't believe in doing things halfway. She had flung herself into being a helpmate to George with the same drive and enthusiasm that characterized all of her life. Then she had paid a price she had never expected. She had lost herself and eventually lost the man she had thought she loved to another woman. No warning. No amicable divorce. Nothing easy, nothing simple to deal with. Just pain, confusion and a loss of direction for her future. But things were different now. Thanks to Cord. The year since the divorce had been hard, but she had made it. She was back on track.

Sighing, Victoria leaned back in her chair. It had been a long but very profitable week for her and the firm. Cord would be pleased. Cord. She smiled a little thinking of her enigmatic boss, her best friend. Even after ten months of working with him, she still found it hard to believe that he had offered her a partnership in Darcourte Architect, Inc. He had been turning away would-be aspirants for a place at his side for years. His reputation for excellence in design had won him quite a few awards, and she was lucky to have him as a mentor. He designed the buildings and she, the setting.

Victoria Wynne, Landscape Architect. Her smile widened at the sign sitting on her file cabinet. Cord had given her the gold-plated set in teak last Christmas. Expensive. Impractical. An ego boost when she needed it so badly. Cord always seemed to know exactly how to get to her, to help, to support, or to just plain irritate her so much that she would fight him for the sheer pleasure of winning.

The intercom buzzed, interrupting her concentration. Still smiling, she reached for it. "Yes, what is it?"

"I need you, Victoria."

Her grin widened at Cord's irritated tone. Something or someone had tweaked the tail of the tiger. Cord's moods varied with the regularity of a thermometer. He kept the whole office on its toes. His temper could have made life difficult, instead it only added spice. Victoria sometimes thought he provoked her for sheer devilment. She would bet her last nickel that what had him going this time were her plans for the current project under construction.

"Am I going to need my armor?" she asked, working at being suitably meek.

"Funny, partner. But I'm not laughing. You put a garden on that section of land I told you I wanted. I want to know why."

Victoria's amusement faded. They had discussed the house in question last week. He had agreed to the modification. "We've already talked about this. We agreed that I could put a terraced garden there and you know it," she reminded him tartly.

"I did not."

Victoria frowned. Cord's memory was nearly photographic in its ability to recall. Beginning to get irritated, she snapped, "All right, I'll be right over." Before he could comment she broke the connection. Face-to-face was the only way to handle this battle. She stalked out of the room, almost barreling into Maybelle as she came down the hall.

The secretary took one look at Victoria's face and grinned. She glanced at her watch. "Right on time.

It's ten o'clock. You two always go at it at ten o'clock. Do you sit in your offices waiting for the right moment?''

"Go away," Victoria muttered. Maybelle knew both her and Cord too well to take offense. "Cord wants my garden and I won't let him have it. You know, for that patio thing he wants." Since the last part of her words coincided with her arrival at Cord's door, he heard her remark.

"Getting reinforcements?" he asked, one dark brow lifted.

Cord dominated the large, airy room. But then there were few things or people Cord wasn't capable of dominating if he chose. Victoria should have been used to the phenomenon but for some reason, today, she was seeing Cord differently. She was seeing the man and not the friend. Vaguely puzzled, but not enough to deflect her from the defense of her terraced garden, she advanced.

"I don't need any reinforcements," she returned smartly, neither of them noticing when Maybelle went about her business.

Cord rose raking his fingers through his hair in frustration. The dark waves with the light sprinkling of silver caught the light, drawing Victoria's eyes. She hadn't noticed the gray before, but she knew she liked it on him. She liked the maturity in his bearing. The mellow richness of his voice, when he wasn't grumping at her, that was.

"Be reasonable, Victoria. I need that patio. The whole line of the house will be spoiled without it."

Victoria perched a hip on his stool, wondering if she were suffering from some sort of spring madness. If she didn't pay attention to the problem at hand, Cord would win. She poked a well-manicured finger at the disputed area of land.

"Look at that ground. You've walked it. You know as well as I do what it will take to make that area level enough for that. My way, the land will be utilized in its natural state. Much cheaper."

Cord glared at her. "I don't work for cheaper. Our clients contract for the best I can give them, and they know it doesn't come for peanuts. I don't compromise on quality."

"I'm not talking about compromise."

"Sounds like it."

Victoria stared down at the drawing. One of them would have to back down. Cord could be as stubborn as she was. He was also brilliant, temperamental, generous, impulsive, loyal, and impossibly protective, especially where she was concerned. Cord was . . . Cord. He made her so angry she could cheerfully have strung him up by his thumbs more times than she cared to count. And yet when she had hit bottom in her life, he had been the one to drag her back to life, kicking and screaming the whole way.

"Victoria get your mind on the job and stop daydreaming," Cord muttered.

She blinked, focusing on his face. Cord was handsome she realized in shock. Oh, not your average picture-pretty handsome but the kind of rugged-strength handsome a woman could depend on. His hair was dark brown, rich, thick with just a few strands of gray. His body was solid, muscled without being muscular. As usual he had the top two buttons of his dress shirt undone and his sleeves rolled up past his elbows. He hated being confined by anything, including the suits his profession as an architect demanded. Her gaze lingered on the dark hair peeking out of the vee at his neck. She could recall every line of his body from the last time they went swimming together. She was momentarily stunned by a strange quiver of need.

Cord? Desire? Her? Since when?

"How long have we known each other?" she murmured. What was wrong with her? she wondered. Cord was her friend. She felt like some love-starved divorcée thinking about him this way.

"Eight years. We met four months before you married George," he replied absently, coming to stand beside her. "Are you all right? You look kind of funny." He put a hand to her forehead. He tried not to notice how satiny smooth her skin felt. He tried to tell himself he wasn't looking for a way to touch her. Lately, it was getting harder not to notice Victoria was a beautiful woman. And available. "You don't seem to have a temperature."

If Victoria had been the kind of person to cry over the irony of a situation, she would have broken down right then. She was sitting beside the most outrageously sexy man she had ever known, a man who was her best friend in the world, a man with whom she had shared all her confidences, a man who had seen her at her worst and not run for cover, and he wanted to know if she was all right. She wasn't. Eight years of friendship had just gone up in smoke. Even now curls of desire were wrapping around her body, resurrecting senses that had been dead since the trauma of her divorce. Her hands clenched, the nails biting into her palms. His touch was calling to her, demanding a response. She fought the spiraling need and concentrated on his face.

"I'm fine." She tried to smile, to reassure him. Her lips felt as if they were straining with the effort.

Cord peered at her, his fingers lingering on her skin. "Are you sure? You've gone white." He took her hand in his, cradling it carefully. Her pride and strength sometimes made him forget she could be hurt. He had held her while she cried over George and then fought her tooth and nail over some scrap of ground for a patio. Friend, coworker and partner. Their relationship had so many facets now that he sometimes wondered if he shouldn't get a road map. "I shouldn't have yelled at you. You were right. The terrace should be there."

"But what about the line of the house?" She could hardly believe her ears. Cord backing down on one of his precious designs.

"I'll think of something else. No sweat." He patted her hand.

The gesture made Victoria feel like his maiden aunt. She wanted to snatch her fingers back but she didn't. Cord was sharp. He would suspect something since he had touched her this way a hundred times or more in the past. He was *always* touching her, she realized. Despite the fact that he was a nontactile person with everyone else, he never missed an opportunity to make physical contact with her. Removing her hand carefully from his grasp, she got to her feet. It was impossible not to notice he stood ready to catch her if necessary.

"I've got work to do," she said quietly, heading for the door.

He watched, worried but trying not to hover. She had been smothered by one man, he wouldn't be the second to take her independence from her. "Why don't you take an early lunch?" he suggested. "Take Maybelle with you if you like. I'll watch the phones."

Victoria glanced at him and then wished she hadn't. He was so dear. Damn him, couldn't he see what had happened to her? She felt as if her whole life had just turned itself inside out. "All right."

Cord frowned at the distracted tone. "But be back at one. A friend of mine is coming in. I'm doing a house for him. I think you should meet him since he's sure to want you to do the grounds." He touched her arm, halting her before she could leave. "I can cancel the appointment if you don't feel up to it. There isn't any rush on this one."

"No. That's fine. I'll see you at one."

Cord let her go. There was no way he could keep her even though he was sure there was something very wrong. "Damn my temper. I shouldn't have yelled at her," he muttered to himself after she left.

He sat down at his desk and fumbled for a cigarette. He was smoking too much these days. Another sign of his dissatisfaction with his life. He leaned his head back, blowing a cloud of smoke into the air. He was lonely and tired of coming home to an empty apartment. His only enjoyment was his time spent here and with Victoria. He needed a diversion, but he hadn't thought of one as yet. No woman really appealed, although he had called an old flame. Darlene had been an enjoyable companion for the evening, but the spark of wanting hadn't been there. He had accepted a nightcap and then made an excuse of an early appointment. Not a satisfactory evening at all. It had left him feeling more jaded, and that annoyed him. He had everything he had worked for. What was wrong with him? Stubbing out his cigarette, he snatched the disputed plans in front of him. Sitting here questioning life was a fool's errand. Work would occupy his mind until whatever weird stage he was going through was over.

Victoria sat down, glad her legs had held up to get her back to her office. She couldn't be attracted to Cord, she told herself. He had never given her the slightest indication that he saw her as a woman. Only a fool would pick out a man that treated her like a favored kid sister. On top of that, there was their friendship. Eight years of history. She couldn't betray it with physical desire. She cared too much about Cord to do that to either of them. But what was she going to do? Maybe if she worked hard enough she could pretend she hadn't noticed how deep his voice was, how it seemed to rumble from somewhere in his chest then pour out like warm honey. Maybe she could pretend she hadn't wanted to touch his bare skin, to taste his lips. She shifted in her chair. X-rated daydreams. Fantasies. She had never had them.

"Fool." She glared at her cluttered desk. She needed a diversion for a late-blooming adolescent mind. She was thirty years old. She could handle a case of good old-fashioned lust with a healthy dose of overwork. "Cord's my friend. That's all he is."

Picking up a pen, she got busy and she stayed that way until Maybelle stopped at her door to tell her it was time to leave for lunch.

"How did you know we were being let out of here together?" Victoria asked, shrugging into the medium-gray jacket that matched her slim skirt.

The gray-haired woman laughed good-naturedly, her brown eyes twinkling. "Cord gave me the good news. I don't know how he's going to cope with the phones. The last time we left him alone in here, he threatened to fire me if I did it again." Maybelle cast a glance at Cord's closed door.

"You shouldn't laugh," Victoria returned, pleased to find that there was only a small quiver of reaction on hearing his name. "Fifteen calls are a lot in an hour. I'm just surprised he didn't pull the phone out of the wall somewhere around the tenth."

"You and me both. All he did was make us promise not to leave him alone again. I'll admit his edict was delivered in a voice a lion would have happily claimed as a full-throated roar. But who's complaining?"

Victoria laughed, feeling her world begin to settle back into place. Maybelle could always be counted on to put things in proper perspective.

The two women exited the building Cord had created for Darcourte Architects, Inc. The modern design, one of Cord's first, fit in with the neighboring structures as though it belonged on one of the older streets in this section of New Orleans. A small courtyard opened to a moderate-sized parking area. Flowers bloomed in a riot of color and fragrance. She had talked Cord into this addition a few months ago when the winter had been especially dreary.

"Let's take my car. I have this really neat place I want to try. Can't get Ralph to go with me." Maybelle led the way to a white station wagon.

"You know your husband prefers your cooking to any restaurant. I don't know why you don't give up trying to turn him into a party animal," Victoria teased. She was feeling better by the moment. Maybe this morning was nothing more than a case of over-active hormones. She had been alone a long time.

"Since our last child left for college, I've been thinking it's time we got out and really enjoyed ourselves. Not like some people I know." She sent Victoria a look.

"Oh, no, you don't. I've heard this lecture before."

"Well, you're going to hear it again. When are you going to stop hibernating? Isn't it about time you joined the human race? There are a lot of sexy, unattached male critters out there. When are you going to cut one out of the herd for yourself, or are you planning on living alone for the rest of your life?"

"I'm happy—"

"Mule feathers," Maybelle interrupted cheerfully, but with determination. "You're existing, moving through time and space by rote. Find a man, Tori. Enjoy yourself. It's time you put that rat, George, behind you. He darn near drained the life right out of you. I swear he was part vampire. But he's gone now, feeding on some other woman, poor soul. Cord may have poked and prodded you in to going back to work for him—heaven only knows why *you* let George talk you in to quitting us in the first place—but you did the hard stuff. You've got that gorgeous apartment."

"Which Cord helped me find."

"New clothes. By the way, did I tell you I like that outfit? Dress for success, I think it's called."

Victoria grinned. Even when Maybelle was on one of her push-Victoria-into-finding-a-man kicks, she could make her smile. "I'm glad it meets with your approval."

"Better yet, it would meet with a male's approval. You've stopped looking like a suburban housewife after taking ten kids to Little League and three dogs to the vet."

Victoria's appreciation of the word picture bubbled over in laughter. Tears were welling in her eyes before she could control herself. "You belong on the stage," she told the older woman when she could breathe again.

"And you belong in some lucky man's bed." Maybelle guided her car into an overcrowded lot. "Darn. Look at this place."

"I have a feeling we'd better find another restaurant or we're both going to be in the suds," she said. "I have to be back by one."

"Nothing doin'. You just tell Cord it was my idea. He owes me fifteen minutes from last night and I always collect my debts."

"You're as bad as he is. You aren't a clock-watcher, so don't pretend to be one. Let's just hope this place has good food and fast service."

They made it back with five minutes to spare.

"See, I told you," Maybelle murmured as she followed Victoria to her office to drop off the morning post.

The intercom buzzed. "My master's voice." Victoria slipped off her jacket before answering. The break with Maybelle had done her good. She was in control again, her voice calm, slightly amused.

"I'm coming," she answered. "Keep your shirt on."

"You're late."

"I'm not. I'm now one minute early and you're using it up with this conversation." This time he was the one to break the connection.

Victoria smiled as she walked across the hall. She was back on track. She could relax.

Cord looked up as she came in. "Lunch did the trick I see."

Victoria paused, realizing she had spoken too soon. The feelings were back, stronger than ever. Only willpower got her across the room and into the chair facing him. His eyes were a deep velvety green, almost evergreen. The faint scent of his after-shave was fresh and minty cool.

"Maybelle took me to a new place." Maybe words would blot out the flickers of desire. Something had to, she thought grimly.

"Would I know it?"

She shook her head, watching his lips, wondering how they would taste. "I don't think so. It just opened." Desperately needing a diversion, she gestured toward the plans on the desk. "Are those the drawings?"

Cord unrolled the paper tube. "These are for James Southerland. You've probably heard me talk about him from time to time. About two months ago he got all fired up to build himself a home. Came to me and this is the result. We're out of the ground now. The studs are up and the roof is on. It's time for the next phase. James wasn't sure what he wanted, so I haven't talked to you about it until now. Thought you could pick his brain today and then get yourself out to the site as soon as your schedule permits for a walk over. Do a workup. You know the routine."

Victoria glanced at the plans, blocking out his appeal as much as she could. She'd never found it so difficult to concentrate on work. "I like this," she murmured after a minute. "Very unusual."

"It has to be. James doesn't like anything that isn't one of a kind." Cord frowned at the plans. "He usually has his mind set exactly on what he wants."

Victoria looked up, hearing something in his voice when he spoke of his friend. "Problems?"

Cord shrugged. "Not ours. His." He leaned back and pulled out a cigarette from his case. "I think you'll like James."

"Is that necessary?" She tipped her head, studying him. Cord was in a strange mood. The intensity of his stare was new. She resisted the urge to fidget.

"No, it's not necessary, but it will happen. Everyone likes James. He can be very charming when he puts his mind to it." He watched her, wondering what she was thinking. Usually he could read her thoughts by the expression in her eyes. Today he could see nothing but beautiful blue mirrors reflecting his own image.

"You're making me nervous." Victoria laughed a little.

"Why?"

She should have known he would pounce on her comment. Her reply was interrupted by Maybelle's soft knock. Victoria concealed her relief at the save.

"Mr. Southerland is here. Shall I show him in?"

"We're ready."

Victoria turned as Cord rose to greet his friend. She studied the man, agreeing with Cord's assessment and adding some of her own. James was handsome with a kind of devil-may-care smile that probably had women falling all over themselves. But it was Cord who held her eyes. His presence was more intense, stronger. James was pepper. Cord was Cajun hot sauce. She smiled at the imagery as Cord made the introductions.

"Cord says you're very good at designing the landscaping for his houses. Are you?" James asked.

Cord glared at him. "Behave James," he warned. "I didn't get Victoria in here for you to bait her."

Victoria shot him a warning look then turned back to James. The days of needing Cord to fight her battles were over. She knew her own worth and wasn't shy about saying so. "Have you ever known Cord to align himself with less than the best?"

James looked surprised at the quick comeback. "No," he admitted slowly, looking at her more carefully.

Victoria stared back, refusing to flinch under the hard-eyed gaze. His slow smile took her by surprise. His faint flicker of admiration made her relax. Whatever the test had been, she had passed.

"Now that that's out of the way, perhaps we could begin," Cord drawled before going to the drafting table. He spread the plans and snapped them into place.

James joined him, Victoria following. Both men went over the design and the few changes Cord had made for the next stage of construction. The house that Cord had designed was one of his best, Victoria decided. The soaring lines and the use of natural materials appealed to her. The way the rooms took advantage of the best exposure was energy conscious without sacrificing comfort. James obviously thought so, too, judging by his comments.

"What do you think, Ms. Wynne?" James turned to her. "Have you any ideas yet?"

"I haven't had a chance to go over the site. I thought I'd take a run out there this afternoon."

James glanced at his watch. "I would like to go out myself, but I have an appointment in twenty minutes. I'll call you when I get back in the office, and we'll set up a time for me to see your ideas."

"As you wish."

A moment later James took his leave.

"He's very controlled, isn't he? He doesn't show his feelings much," she said, watching Cord as he rolled up the house plans. "I get the feeling that what you see is only a small portion of the man."

Cord gave her a sharp look. "Right on both counts. James doesn't like temperament in people. He believes in channeling all his energy into getting to a specific goal. I'm glad he's not a competitor of mine."

"Oh, I don't know. You'd give him a run for his money," she said, the teasing rejoinder holding more emotion than she wanted him to know. She laughed to cover the intensity. "It's difficult believing you two are friends."

He grimaced slightly, acknowledging the comment. "Actually we're more like brothers. Don't know why. We met through a friend of his for whom I designed a house."

"There are some similarities."

"Success. Drive. Ambition." He shrugged. "Not much else. He's looking for a family, a wife. I'm not. He likes calm and peace. I get bored. He likes the push and pull of business, I hate it." He dropped into a chair and pulled out a cigarette. Blowing a small cloud of smoke, he watched her through it. "Why the sudden interest? You've never paid any attention to one of our clients before."

Cord looked at her as though he would see into her soul. At one time she had nothing to hide. But no longer.

"No reason." She shrugged, pretending indifference. She couldn't tell him that she had been curious about the man he called a friend. Cord was a loner, passionately devoted to his privacy. She could count on one hand the number of people who were important to him or that he confided in. Even as close as she was to Cord, she knew next to nothing about his past.

"I told you he could be charming. You wouldn't be thinking of trying your luck, would you?" He took another drag on the cigarette, the tobacco biting into his tongue.

"My luck?" Surely he couldn't mean what she thought.

"You know. Dating."

He *did* mean it. The knowledge hurt. The sensation was as confusing as the rest of her unwanted feelings. "Why not? He's an attractive man. You've been telling me to get out more."

Cord stubbed out the cigarette with a swift movement, then leaned forward in his chair. "You shouldn't start with him. He's not an easy man de-

spite that charm. He's just gotten out of a relationship that has left him raw. His redheaded woman took
another man, so he isn't in the mood to be kind. Mess
with him and you're going to be hurt.''

Victoria didn't know whether to laugh or cry. The
last thing she wanted was to be involved with anyone.
And how could she be attracted to another man when
right now she was seeing only Cord? Blast his blind-
ness—and her stupidity.

"My responsibility." The words escaped, an un-
conscious challenge, a prod to masculine interest if
there were any to be found.

Cord held on to his temper with effort. "Are you so
blind that you'll walk into another George situation?
If you went out with James, he'd only be using you for
a substitute."

Angered at the reference and the way he presumed
she needed his big-brother guidance in this part of her
life, Victoria got to her feet, her hands planted on her
hips. "For your information, I hadn't thought about
going out with him, and heaven knows, I doubt he's
thought about asking if all you say is true. But I'll tell
you this, if he did ask me out, I might just go. He's a
nice man. And your friend." She grabbed her sketch-
pad and pencil. "Sometimes, Cord, you go too far.
You've helped me more than I can ever repay, but I
never gave you the right to check out the men in my
life. I will go out with whom I choose and where I
choose."

Cord stood up, glaring at her across the desk that
divided them. "You need a keeper."

"Says who?" Her eyes flashed fire. If she had been
a woman to throw things, she would have thrown her
pad at him.

"No one has to say it, the past speaks for itself."

She stiffened at the reference. His face altered in a second, contrition stealing the anger. Victoria turned and started for the door, intending to escape. He caught her before she reached it.

"I'm sorry," he whispered, fighting her when she would have pulled out of his hold.

Victoria twisted but couldn't break free. Inky strands of hair slipped the bounds of the braid. Her emotions were in chaos. All the safety, the security, the warmth of their past was shattered. Nothing was the same anymore. They had hurt each other.

"Talk to me, Victoria."

The plea reached her as the apology had not. She froze, then slowly turned to him. She was wary, uneasy, for Cord never pleaded for anything. He drove through life taking and giving with equal energy.

"What's happening to us?" she whispered.

He touched her cheek, smoothing the hair back in place. "You're coming alive again. I've been waiting, but now I find I miss having you depend on me and living just for your career." He spoke softly, his voice deep and slow . "I don't want to lose you."

If he but knew. "You won't." It was her turn to touch him. She turned her lips into his palm. His sharp intake of breath startled her but not as much as the swift way he released her.

"Don't."

Her eyes filled. Rejection. Cord? Her hands clenched. "I have to go." She fumbled at the knob, finally yanking the door open. She could feel him watching although he said nothing. He just let her go.

Two

Victoria unclipped the plans from the drafting table, rolling them carefully before sliding them into the protective cylinder for storage. She was tired, bone weary. Fighting her emotions, guarding her words, being at odds with Cord was sapping her energy. It was late, almost time to go home. She glanced at the closed door across the hall. He was there, holed up in his office, growling at anyone who came near. She had wanted to talk to him about the Southerland project, but the words they had spoken, the way he had pushed her away, hung between them. She didn't know how to put things right.

Sighing, she got up and went to the window, leaning her forehead against the windowpane to look out. She had been to the Southerland site, walked the grounds and admired the house that Cord had designed. A home really. The kind of place a man could build a life with a woman. Cord had a gift for creating a sanctuary, a place of rest, relaxation and safety. His home in the bayou was a perfect example. But no one shared his life or his home.

Cord. Her mind shied from his name. Just thinking about him brought a sting of tears to her eyes. Work. Her balance. The leveler that made living possible in impossible situations. If she could just block her mind long enough, maybe she could stop seeing the man and go back to knowing the friend. She had to try before she lost him.

The phone rang. It was James.

"I'm sorry I'm so late getting back to you. My appointment ran over. Did you have an opportunity to go out to the site?"

She pulled herself together enough to answer. "I did. I have some ideas that I'd like to run by you before I start on the preliminary sketches."

"Good. I'm going to be really busy for the next few days. Would it be possible for us to get together tonight? Over dinner, perhaps?"

Victoria hesitated, then felt like a fool. She had accepted many such invitations without a second thought. But because of Cord and what he had told her about James, she was vacillating like a teenager. "What time?"

"Seven?"

"That's fine," Victoria replied. She and James made arrangements to meet before she hung up.

Cord stood at the door watching Victoria. He had come to apologize once again. He hated being at odds with her. They fought constantly, but they both enjoyed it and there was no real damage in their battles. But this time things had gotten out of hand. He had hurt her when he had meant only to protect. So he had come to explain the unexplainable and had listened, instead, to her making a date with James.

"You won't listen will you?" he said roughly, coming into the room.

Victoria started, glancing over her shoulder. Usually she had a special built-in radar where Cord was concerned, despite his characteristic cat-footed approaches. "What are you talking about?"

"I heard you on the phone just now."

She tensed but tried not to show it. She couldn't take another argument, but it looked as if she wouldn't be given a choice. "Eavesdropping?"

His lips tightened but he didn't respond. There were more important matters. "Are you really going out with him?"

She watched him carefully. "Why does it matter so much to you who I go out with? I'm over twenty-one." A faint hope flickered. Could he be jealous?

Cord sighed wearily. He knew her in this mood. She could be stubborn and had a pride to match his own. "Do whatever you want. But just remember this. That man's got more notches on his bed than Don Juan. You're so damn innocent it hurts. You're out of your league, honey." Even as he said the words, he wished he had kept his mouth shut. He knew Victoria, knew he was speaking out of his own damnable black jealousy, emotion he had no right to feel. Yet he couldn't stop himself.

Victoria inhaled sharply at the thrust. Cord could be a bear when he was in a temper, but until now he'd never been cruel. The elation that her foolish emotions had created fizzled like a pricked balloon. "How would you know what my league is? You've never seen me as anything but your personal charity case," she retaliated, hurting and lashing back.

"Somebody had to take you on. It's a damn sure thing that your family wouldn't when that husband of yours dropped you flat. And you sure weren't doing a thing to help yourself. You weren't much more than a limp rag when I got to you. You let that damn fool flatten every inch of you that threatened his masculinity."

"So enter Cord to the rescue. A swearing, chainsmoking, hard-driving knight in tarnished armor." The sarcasm was honey and poison dipped. The soft New Orleans drawl made the words even more powerful.

"I never asked to be a knight."

"I never asked to be rescued."

Evergreen eyes looked into Victoria's face, dissecting each reaction, probing for a weak point. She stood her ground. She had never backed down from Cord. Others might quell before his moods, but he had never frightened her. The gentleness, the tender bully who had pushed her back to life was gone. This man demanded from her in ways that were new.

"I am no man's notch," she stated, needing to say something. How could he have said that to her? He knew her so well and still believed that of her? "I value myself higher than that."

"You will be his." He would not compromise. He had not saved her, after the mess that jerk she had married had made of her, to see her hurt by a man like James.

"He's on the make and he's hungry," he continued. "I didn't break a confidence on the man's personal life for the fun of it. Didn't you hear me? The woman he's been going with left him. He wants a replacement. He's hurting and he might not care if you get hurt in the process." James and he went back a long way despite the five-years' difference in their ages. Only for Victoria would he betray his friend. "Break the date. If you want to go out, if you have decided to rejoin the ranks of the singles, start with someone who won't hurt you."

"Who? Don't tell me you've got someone all picked out for me. You found me the apartment I live in and talked me into becoming your partner when you have been actively refusing to take anyone into the firm for quite a number of years. Why should you stop at choosing the man to succeed George?"

Cord's fists clenched at his sides. A different kind of pain lanced his chest. Anger died. Weariness won the battle. Without a word, he turned and stalked out. To stay was to speak words that were better left unsaid. He was already bleeding from the wounds Victoria had inflicted.

Victoria stared at the door, appalled at herself. The hurt in Cord's eyes would haunt her. How could she have said anything so unforgivable? Her feet were moving before she had time to consider her course. She couldn't let this awful fight go on a second longer than it took for her to beg his forgiveness. She burst into his office, stopping short when she saw him slumped in the chair behind his desk. His head was in his hands. Cord was an unstoppable force, never vanquished, never weary. But he looked that way now and she had done it to him.

"Go away, Tori. We'll talk tomorrow when we're both calmer. Enjoy your date."

Her hands lifted then dropped. His voice was so lifeless, empty. He never, ever called her Tori. He hated the nickname. "Cord, look at me."

"No. I mean it. Go home. Now!"

She took a step back then halted. "No, I won't be driven away." Eight strides carried her to his side. She yanked his hands down. "Look at me. I came to apologize. I had no right. To you of all the people in the world, I had no right to speak that way. I know you wouldn't pick a man for me. You have never forced me to do anything." Still he wouldn't look at her. Tears started in her eyes. Frustrated, she went down on her knees beside him. He lifted his head, then. She wished he hadn't. This man she didn't know. This man held hell in his eyes.

Cord lifted his fingers to her cheek where the silver streams flowed for him. He touched the tears, dipping into the liquid to carry it to his mouth. A sensual gesture, even a sexual one, though he did not mean it that way. "For me? I don't think anyone has ever cried for me."

"For us." She was afraid to move. She had almost lost him. She knew it as sure as she knew the sun would rise tomorrow. "I hurt us both. I didn't mean to."

"I," he hesitated. He had never told her how much she meant to him. Trusting was not something that came easily to him. But he trusted Victoria. She had

hurt him. For the first time in their relationship she
had brought him pain he hadn't been able to handle.
"I care about you." His hand cradled her cheek,
smoothing the silken skin, absorbing the warmth in
the only way he allowed himself. "I don't want to see
you hurt. When you first worked for me, you were a
beautiful woman with fire in her eyes. You tilted that
chin and dared me not to hire you. Not many men
would have faced me that way. I respected and admired your strength. I liked your mind and the drive
that took you to the head of your class. You had
George. You were engaged. Slowly, I watched him
douse the bright flame inside you. You left me and the
business after you married him. You became a shadow
of his needs and wants. George almost destroyed you,
and I don't want to see you hurt again. I stood by
once. I can't this time."

"I'm not asking you to stand by and James can't
hurt me that way." Even as she said the words, the
irony of them touched her. It was Cord she wanted,
not James.

"I'm not a foolishly naive virgin anymore. George
tore the blinders off. I know what I want and what
you've given me," she said, the words spilling out in
an impassioned torrent.

Cord shook his head sadly. "I gave you nothing. It
was you who gave to me. I know that I can make
buildings that sing. But you make the setting. Until
you, there was no one I wanted to trust to create the
environment for my work. I can talk to you when I
can't to anyone else. I don't have to wonder if you
want something from me." His other hand came up to
cup her face. "I guess what I'm trying to say is I was

jealous." He made himself smile. The gesture cost him more than he thought he had to give, but he succeeded.

Victoria searched his expression. Cord and she shared honesty, but this time she felt there was something he held back, something vital. Yesterday she would have asked, demanded if necessary, what was being edited. Today she was afraid. Her fingers encircled his wrists where his pulse throbbed with life.

"You have no reason to be jealous of any man. I care for you, too. You must know that." Her smile was as strained as his. The bond of friendship was stretched to the limit, but she would not allow it to break. Cord was the mainstay of her life. "But you're right. I can't keep hiding. A year is a long time. I'll try to get out." Even though you've made it clear that you're unavailable to me, she added silently. The very thing that binds us, separates us.

Cord hated the gratitude he knew she felt, but he had stopped fighting it. Instead he concentrated on the trust she gave him, the confidences they had shared, the pieces of her life interwoven with his own. He knew he could tie her to him with a word but then neither of them would be free ever again.

"So try, honey. Go let James wine you and dine you." He brushed his thumbs softly over her lips, stilling the words he saw forming. "Just remember this, tarnished armor or not, I'll break every bone in his hands if he hurts you. So make sure you play fair. He's my friend too."

Relieved, Victoria relaxed back on her heels. Her friend was back in all his fire-breathing glory. Afraid to risk the tentative peace with a real explanation of her "date," she gave him the truth. "I promise I won't trip him and beat him to the floor."

Cord dipped his head as he hunted for a cigarette and a lighter. He needed something to keep his hands busy. Victoria leaned across him to open his desk drawer and extract a book of matches. She struck one and held it to the cigarette.

"You should stop smoking."

He cupped his hands around hers. For one moment their eyes locked. Hers, hesitant, needing reassurance. His, dark, full of secrets. "Stop worrying. Every man has to die from something."

"A world without Cord. What would I do?"

Her words were sweet, filling him with warmth after their storm. She cared about him. He needed to know that, but he masked the need beneath the banter he had perfected so long ago. "Go, woman. The man's not likely to enjoy being kept waiting even for a woman as beautiful as you." He blew out the match.

Victoria tossed the book back into the drawer and rose. "And what are you doing tonight? Going out with the deliciously decadent Darlene?" Cord laughed as she had hoped he would. The words tore at her, but he wouldn't know that.

He leaned back in his chair, watching her. "Now I wonder why you pick on Darlene? She's a nice woman."

Victoria scowled. "Only to the male of the species." Of all Cord's ladies, Darlene was the first to rate a repeat performance. Victoria didn't want to think what that meant.

"Well, I wouldn't be dating her if she was turned on by her own kind," he drawled. "Tell you what. Let's fix James and Darlene up together."

Victoria recognized the game they played. Cord was probing. She had given him enough. It was time to have a little pride. "No way. That woman has claws. You're the only man I know who can take her on without coming away skinned." She strolled to the door, his rich humor surrounding her.

"Honey, I do believe that's the nicest thing you've said to me in a long time."

"Fiddle." Victoria turned when she reached the door. "Cordell Jackson Darcourte, that was not a compliment and you know it."

"Was too."

He was riding a high. Victoria had taken him to hell and lifted him to heaven, and she didn't even know it. Her flounce was a masterpiece. The emptiness of his office when she stomped down the hall to her own was almost worth it. So James would be raked over by Darlene and he wouldn't. Pride and a kind of male superiority filled him. Damn. He could give James quite a few years. There was still life in the old boy, after all. He grinned, inhaling more than he should have when smoking. The result was a coughing spell that made him throw the cigarette into the ashtray.

"Damn things. It's time to quit." He glared at the white tube. His grin reappeared and widened. Victoria wanted him to quit. He'd do it just to see her face and watch her cope with his temper. He knew himself well. Quitting was not going to have a beneficial effect on his personality, but then very few things did. As for Darlene, it would be interesting to see how she would react to her would-be lover in the throes of a nicotine fit. A grin became outright laughter. He wondered which of them had the longest claws and the most staying power. So far he had escaped Darlene's favorite ploys for capture. His tactics were driving her wild. If he had been in the mood for a rerun affair, he would be in the perfect position to call the shots.

Victoria heard the laughter and wondered at the cause. Gathering her handbag and umbrella, she left her office. A frown pleated her brows as she considered Cord's temperament of late. To her knowledge, Cord had never been a womanizer. His relationships were flexible but not numerous. He dated the woman of his choice for a time then parted, leaving behind a friend of sorts. None had succeeded in recapturing his interest until Darlene. She wondered if Cord could be getting serious about Darlene. Had he suddenly decided to take a leap into a committed relationship? Was that why he seemed so unlike himself? For a man like him, a change of that kind would be difficult. Brilliant, demanding, but totally honest about himself, he would realize he had to compromise to live with someone. He would fight it and the reasons for its existence.

Lost in her thoughts, Victoria hardly noticed the drive home. It was only when she entered her apartment and caught sight of the clock that she realized how late it was. James would be arriving shortly. Normally neat to the point of a fetish, tonight, Victoria tossed her clothes off and hurried into a shower. A blue silk gown the color of her eyes was her choice for the evening. Onyx dangle earrings and a bracelet to match were her only jewelry. Understatement in clothes and makeup had always suited her. Swirling her hair atop her head in a style that looked easy but wasn't, she finished dressing. A spritzer of cologne and she was ready just in time. The doorbell rang. She took a deep breath and one last look in the mirror before she went to let James in.

"Sorry I'm late. You would be a prompt woman." He walked past her, smiling a little.

Victoria grinned back. The light, breezy opening was just the icebreaker she needed. No intensity, no pressure. "What would you have said if I hadn't been ready?"

"Nothing." He glanced around the apartment with interest. "I like your home," he commented. "Although it doesn't look much as I expected."

"I'm almost afraid to ask what you were expecting."

"Artsy stuff. Not a nice clutter that says a person lives here. Not a bit of beauty mixed in with the practical. It appeals to me. You wouldn't like to recommend an interior decorator for my place, would you? Someone who could do something similar for me."

"I'm responsible for the clutter," she said, looking at her home with new eyes. "But I do know a decorator you might like."

"Good." He picked up the jacket lying on the back of the sofa and held it out. "Are we ready?"

Victoria let him help her, silently marveling at how easy it was to be with him. He was just another man to her. Attractive, nice in an abrupt sort of way, but nothing to stir her senses. His light hand at the base of her spine as he followed her out the door did nothing to or for her. Cord had been way off base.

On the heels of that thought came another. If James, who appealed to most women, didn't stir her senses then she was in deeper trouble than she'd first thought with her response to Cord. It wasn't her solitary life-style causing her reactions to Cord. It was something else, which was not a reassuring conclusion. In fact, a frightening one.

"Is Galatoire's all right? I made reservations, but we can go somewhere else if you prefer."

"One of my favorite places."

"Good. So tell me about the site. Did you like it?"

Victoria leaned back determined to enjoy herself. If she concentrated on business and the man beside her maybe she could blot out Cord, for the moment at least. "It's a beautiful piece of property. Did you want to keep the character intact or tame it?"

"Tame as in boxed hedges and hothouse flowers?"

Startled at the description, Victoria stared at him. "You are kidding, I hope. Tamed to me, means smoothing the land, creating settings. I don't box hedges or, at least, not often."

He chuckled at the decisive answer. "Good. I hate hedges. I want to see the land, I don't want to rape it. But neither do I wish to take my life in my hands walking around it."

"I have a feeling it's going to take a bit of doing to come up with something that satisfies you," she murmured.

"You should be used to picky males after working with Cord."

"I should, but I can live in hope that one of you is reasonable," she replied, momentarily forgetting that

James had a reputation for toughness and she didn't know him well enough to tease.

"I am always reasonable." He slanted her a glance. "You'll see. Being unreasonable takes too much time and energy."

Three

———

I love this place." Victoria glanced around Galatoire's Restaurant. Described by the locals as a glori-
fied barbershop, Galatoire's more than lived up to its
reputation. Bright overhead lights and mirror-lined
walls made dining a bit campy and fun rather than intimate. She and Cord had eaten here many times, but
she didn't want to remember that.

"I don't come here often," James admitted.

There was nothing she could say to that without
sounding too familiar. The waiter approached, taking
the need for a comment. When they were alone again,
Victoria asked, "Do you have any special likes and
dislikes in the plant-and-tree line?" There was a faint
itching sensation at the nape of her neck, almost as
though someone were watching her. She looked dis-

creetly about, seeing no one she knew. Shrugging the feeling away, she tried to concentrate on business.

"You want to talk business before we eat?" James asked.

Victoria looked up, surprised that he'd asked. "It's why we're here." Her voice was soft, despite its decisiveness.

He laughed. "I like your honesty." He leaned forward slightly. "So tell me what I should have on my grounds. And forget the likes and dislikes. I've already told you the only one."

"Boxed hedges," she finished for him, smiling at him. She reached up to touch the base of her neck, wondering if she were paranoid. Someone was definitely watching her or else she had an allergy that was coming out in an itchy rash. Distracted, she glanced around and still saw nothing. Fortunately, James didn't notice.

"Have you got any drawings yet?"

They paused as the waiter brought their food. The conversation resumed almost immediately.

"A few ideas, a sketch or two that I brought home from the office. If you don't mind taking a few minutes when you drop me off, I'll show you what I have and you can give me an opinion. It'll save you a trip back to the office."

"Sounds good to me, but I didn't really expect you to go to this much trouble. I was in a rush when I started the house, but I'm not anymore."

It didn't take much intelligence to realize James's new house and the breakup of his relationship were somehow related. Up close Victoria could see the pain in his eyes, but it hadn't made him cruel or cynical.

She found herself liking the man for his quiet acceptance of the blow life had dealt him.

"It's no trouble. I enjoy my work. Sometimes I get carried away with some of Cord's designs. I do a little overtime. Yours is one of his best."

Across the room, Cord watched James and Victoria laughing, talking as they shared a meal. He had chosen Galatoire's because he hadn't wanted to closet himself with Darlene in an intimate restaurant. But he would rather have dealt with Darlene and a romantic setting than sit by while James wined and dined Victoria. She was smiling at James, looking so beautiful in that silk bit of nothing that she made every other woman in the place, including Darlene, look overdressed. James touched her, damn him. It was the first date. He hadn't needed to touch her hand. Didn't the man have any finesse at all? Cord glared at them, frustrated, irritated, and angry at himself for both emotions.

"Cord, you aren't listening to me," Darlene accused, her green eyes narrowing in temper. "In fact, you haven't been listening to me at all this evening. I'm not used to being ignored."

Cord made himself smile as he focused on Darlene's petulant face. As usual, she was dressed to send a man's blood pressure to the danger level. He should have been affected, but all he could think was that he hoped she didn't take too deep a breath or that the designer believed in superglue in strategic places.

"I know very well what you're used to, pet." He took her hand and carried it to his lips, feeling guilty. Her gown wasn't really that low-cut. She gave him her best sultry smile, and he felt like a fraud. A discreet glance at his watch told him it was too early to end the evening. He cursed silently.

"I tell you what, why don't I take you dancing?" he asked. Darlene loved to dance. He wouldn't enjoy himself, but it would make her happy. She was an interesting companion and they had shared some good times in the past.

"Do you mean it? I know you hate it."

He needed to get out of the restaurant. "I mean it. You can even pick the place." He got to his feet and tossed some bills onto the table. His hand on Darlene's arm, he guided her toward Victoria's table. He had no choice in the route, not that he would have taken another if he had.

"Enjoying yourselves?" he asked, stopping beside Victoria. Her start and the swift turn of her head conveyed her surprise.

James smiled. "I didn't see you. Sorry. Want to join us?"

Cord glanced at him, trying to hide his irritation and knowing at the change in James's expression that he hadn't succeeded. The sharp look James sent Victoria went unnoticed by her.

No wonder she had felt someone watching her. "I didn't know you were here," Victoria said, avoiding as much as she could seeing the red-tipped nails wrapped around Cord's arm. Politeness demanded she acknowledge Darlene but nothing could make her smile genuine.

"We're just on our way out. How about you?" Cord probed cautiously.

"A few minutes for us as well. Victoria has some drawings at her place for the landscaping she wants to show me."

Darlene slanted Victoria a sly look. "I thought it was etchings, darling."

Victoria held on to her temper only because they were in a public place. Darlene had never liked her and always made a point of taking free shots whenever the opportunity arose.

"Behave, pet," Cord said, annoyed at the dig even though the thought had run through his own mind. He wanted to believe it was his temper thinking, not truth. "We'll leave you to it. Don't forget, you have an early appointment tomorrow." He laid his free hand on Victoria's bare shoulder, needing to touch her if only for a moment.

Victoria shrugged lightly, although inside she was seething. Cord was acting like a heavy-handed brother. She knew her schedule better than he did, and she had never missed an appointment in her career and he knew it.

"I'll be there," she managed, feeling as though she were spitting the words out. James's chuckle as Cord and Darlene left was a spur to her temper.

"I don't believe it." He leaned back in his chair, watching Victoria. "You look like you're going to explode."

"I feel like it," she admitted.

"Why?"

"I would have thought that would be obvious."

"It should be. I know Cord, and I'm beginning to know you. But my instincts tell me that all is not what it seems. What game are you and Cord playing? Dar-

lene doesn't look like a very happy lady. Cord acts as
if he'd like to separate my head from my shoulders,
and you jumped as if you had seen a ghost." His eyes
narrowed as he studied her. "This may be a bit con-
ceited of me, but did you set me up to make him jealous?"

"I don't play games like that." Angered, Victoria
picked up her bag and started to get up. James stopped
her with a hand over hers.

"I'm sorry. You're getting the fallout from my
feelings about someone else."

Victoria's anger died. His pain was a living thing.
She could understand the feeling. "My fault, too. I'm
touchy right now." She leaned back.

"Cord?"

She almost lied then changed her mind. "Does it
show?"

"No. I'm guessing more than anything else. I'd offer to help, but I'd be the last person to advise you."

"There isn't anything I can do anyway. It's on my
side, not his."

James frowned. "Are you sure? He looked too angry for there not to be something."

"Protectiveness. He knows what a mess I was in
after my divorce. You know Cord. He gets one idea in
his mind and he won't budge." She shook her head. "I
can't believe I'm telling you all of this."

"Misery loves company. Do you want to go home
now? We can see the plans in the office tomorrow if
you like."

Victoria rose with him. "No. I'd rather do them tonight."

He smiled a little grimly. "Work does make a halfway decent antidote."

They walked without touching to the foyer. A couple came in just as they reached the door. The light shone on a fiery mane of red hair. Victoria watched as James froze. This must be the woman who had left him. She turned, seeing James. The man at her side slipped an arm about her waist as she brushed past them. The meeting was over in seconds. Victoria watched James watching the pair take a table.

"That's her, isn't it?"

"Yes." He stared at them for a moment then turned away. "Let's go." He took Victoria's arm.

"We're a fine pair, you and I," she murmured, respecting him enough not to probe.

"If I didn't feel like I had been run over by a truck, I'd disagree with you," he muttered, urging her into the car.

"Was that the man?"

"Yes." The engine roared to life.

"It's my turn to ask if you'd rather skip tonight."

"My answer is the same as yours."

Victoria inclined her head with a sigh. Two lonely people. Both wanting someone else and settling for business and the whiling away of a few hours of darkness, working.

Cord sprawled carelessly in the chair. A decanter of brandy stood on the table at his elbow. An ashtray, empty, sat beside, it. He held an unlit cigarette, rolling it restlessly between his thumb and forefinger as he watched the rain drip down the window. Tonight had been a disaster. If he had planned it that way, he couldn't have done a better job. Darlene was furious with him. And she had a right to be, he acknowledged. After all, it had been he who had approached her a few weeks ago. They had been lovers once. There was no reason for her to suspect that he had simply wanted and needed a companion for the occasional evening. An indifferent companion for the most part.

Putting the cigarette between his lips, he tasted the bite of the tobacco on his tongue. He wanted a smoke. Once he was able to find his lighter, he started to light up. The flame was a scant inch away from the tip when he changed his mind. Smoking because he wanted to was one thing. Smoking because he needed it was unacceptable. The resolve to quit hardened. Closing the lighter he tossed it onto the floor. The cigarette followed. He swore hard and vehemently.

"Women!"

He glared at the rain and then the brandy. He had yet to take a drink. The way he felt right now he would get rip-roaring drunk, and he had never liked being that deep under the influence. Getting up, he paced to the window and back. Energy flowed through him, demanding release, but there was none. He'd be forty next month. Was this the midlife crisis men spoke of? Was this the time in his life when he looked back and wondered if he had made the right decisions, chosen the right path for his life? He hated introspection, poking in the shadows of his past. There was nothing back there he wanted to remember. He had had no childhood, nothing but work, school and responsibilities a man would have found difficult.

His divorced mother had worked too long and too hard, with no one to help but him, no one to play the father in the house to his younger, by three years, brother. He'd been a parent when he had been little more than a child himself. Even now he could taste the defeat of not being able to stop Robert from doing wrong. Even now he could remember his mother's tears as she sat at the bare kitchen table and cried out her heartbreak because her baby was in jail. Nothing he had done had been enough. She had blamed him. He knew now it had been her guilt talking, but the scars remained. So many scars.

At one time he had tried to pretend his background had no bearing on the man he had made of himself. He had learned better. There were always people around looking for a weapon to use against those more successful than themselves. Gossip in his business, especially the kind that followed his con-artist brother, was a tainted image he could not afford. Many of his projects were for people of power and wealth, people who had to have complete faith in his honesty. Sighing deeply, he turned from the window, knowing it was useless to worry about what could not be changed. He had protected himself and his business the best he could.

His thoughts focused on Victoria. Maybe here he could make a change. He knew where the problem lay, the reason he had been in a rotten mood for the last few months. Victoria. The woman, not the friend. He knew to the moment when he had seen her as the desirable creature she was. It had happened the second day after he had taken her to his house on the bayou. She had needed a place to hide, to lick the wounds George had inflicted. He had taken her home with him, never suspecting that having her there would turn his own life upside down. A thunderstorm. A nightmare. A soft body still warm from sleep. He had held her when she had cried those first tears of release. He had stared out the window at the lightning shooting across the sky and fought the desire that had sprung out of nowhere. He had hated himself for thinking of her as a woman when she needed a friend so much. He had hated noticing how beautifully her body fit to his, how enticing she had looked in the thin gown that clung to her deliciously curved form.

He had stayed through the week with her, noticing more each day but learning to live with the desire. She saw him as nothing but a friend. She needed his support for she had no one else to help her. George had seen to that by systematically cutting her ties with old friends, even making it impossible for her to keep her job with his firm as a junior associate. The fire and the drive that had brought her to his office, hunting a job four days after her graduation from college, had been quenched by the rat she'd married. He had wanted to help her find that flame again. He had admired and respected her ambition and her determination. And he had succeeded when she had taken the partnership he had offered her. Cord smiled a little grimly, remembering her pleasure. He knew she hadn't expected it. Even now he wasn't sure why he had been willing to share it with her when he could think of no one else he would have offered a piece of his life. There were so many things he didn't understand about his relationship with Victoria, so many facets that created emotions he didn't want to understand. He liked his life simple. Victoria was far from simple.

* * *

Victoria hung up her raincoat on the coat tree just inside her office door. Glancing out the window, she shook her head. Another dreary day. They needed the rain; the summer had been exceptionally dry. But she could have used a sunny day for a bit of silent moral support. For the first time since she had come to work for Darcourte, she wished she were home. She didn't want to face Cord. She didn't want to remember seeing him with Darlene or recall the way he had spoken to her. He had embarrassed her and given James a crazy idea about their relationship. But she had no choice but to face him—unless she intended running forever. And she had worked too hard to run, fought pain and loss to build a new place, a new image. So she had put on her clothes and pretended that this was just another day.

Taking out the plans for the site she intended to visit this morning, she studied them. A door slammed. Cord's. She didn't lift her head even when she heard his footsteps stop in her doorway.

Cord stared at her. She was ignoring him. He knew the signs, although she only used the tactic under extreme provocation. "Well, did you enjoy yourself?" He tried for neutrality but failed.

"I had a nice time." Victoria didn't look up.

He took a step closer, shutting the door behind him. "Look at me."

"Why?"

"Why not? Are you hiding something?"

Her chin came up, her eyes alight. "No, I'm just busy. You're the one who reminded me of my early appointment last night."

Cord crossed to stand in front of the desk. The solid barrier was more flimsy than her pride. "I shouldn't have done that," he admitted.

"No, you shouldn't have. When have I ever let you or this firm down?"

"Never—"

But once started, her words tumbled out, rushing over his comment as though it didn't exist. "Even after you bullied me in to coming back here, even when I had trouble deciding what to buy for lunch, I still did good work."

"I know that." He wanted to wrap his arms around her and just hold her. He had hurt her. He knew the value she placed on her career. In many ways it had become her family. He understood, for it was the same for him.

She breathed deeply, appalled at her lack of control. A hundred words swirled in her mind, but none made sense. None conveyed her confusion, her need to understand the changes that were demanding new emotions and behaviors. She desperately wanted their former stable relationship back. She didn't want to see the man instead of the friend. She didn't want to look at him right now and wish that she were in his arms, that his mouth was fitted to hers, that his hands were stroking her bare skin. She wanted him to want her, not Darlene. The thought of Cord holding Darlene, making love to her, made Victoria ill. The fun and excitement of battling with Cord was gone. In its place were guards and defenses against hurt.

"I don't understand you anymore." She spoke softly, tentatively, needing to find a way back.

Cord watched her, studying her reactions. "Are you sure it isn't yourself?"

Her eyes widened. He knew. The heat ran under her skin, tinting her cheeks red. She didn't know where to look. She wanted to hide. As if he read the wish, Cord came around the desk and took her hands.

"There's nothing wrong with what's happening to you. Just let it be. I'm still here. I'm not going anywhere. I know I haven't been acting sanely where you're concerned..." He tried a laugh. Even to his own ears it sounded rusty. "I want you to be happy. If James..."

Victoria almost sagged in relief. He didn't know. "It isn't James. The only thing we were doing last night was discussing the landscaping. He took me home, came in, and we spent two hours knocking around ideas. If I had gotten undressed and danced on the table, I doubt he would have noticed. You were right about his lover and about him. I would have told you yesterday, but you were so angry, and then when you weren't I was afraid to."

Cord drew back, staring at her. He felt as though he had taken two blows to the chest. One, the most important one, was she didn't want James. He left that part unsaid. "You were afraid of me? Why? My temper certainly never bothered you before."

Victoria wrapped her fingers around his wrists, holding him when he would have pulled away. "Tell me what Darlene means to you." She had answered him about James, it was his turn.

Startled, wary, Cord looked at their hands. "Why do you ask?"

"The same reason you asked me about James."

"You know who she is to me."

"Is or was?"

He pulled his hands free and raked his fingers through his hair. "I need a cigarette," he grumbled, wishing he hadn't left his last pack at home out of temptation's way. He glanced at her to find her waiting for an answer. "You are part bulldog."

She wouldn't be sidetracked. "What's good for the goose is—"

"Good for the gander," he finished the proverb irritably.

"You aren't going to answer are you?"

"No."

She frowned at the bite in his tone. He looked ready to hit something. "Are you all right? You haven't been acting yourself lately."

Cord laughed grimly. "And you don't know why." He started for the door. A man could stand just so much from the woman he wanted so badly he could taste it, and whom he was determined not to take. "You've got an agile mind. Think." Without another word, he walked out, leaving her with her thoughts.

Victoria was shocked at the bitterness in his words. Cord could be and was many things, but he had never been bitter. He had sounded almost as though he resented her. Yet why? What was it that he implied was so obvious that she was missing it? Hardly realizing what she was doing, she gathered her plans together. She had to get out of there. He hadn't answered her about Darlene. Was that a clue or was Cord just being protective of the woman he dated? Both seemed equally possible. He had seemed to know what was wrong with her, and yet he had the wrong man attached to the problem. Another clue? She shook her head as she got into her car to drive to the construction site. Instead of helping her sort out her feelings, his remarks only clouded the issue. A headache built to match the ache of desire that seemed to have taken permanent root in her body.

She couldn't keep going this way. She had to get things into perspective. The drive out of town had provided a much needed break. Her head still ached but not as badly. Victoria inhaled the rain-clean fragrance of the country air. The sun had decided to finally make its appearance after three days of hide and seek. Easing the car to a stop before a once impressive Old South home, she sat looking at the dilapidated building.

Getting out of the car, she surveyed the house before her. A long gallery, running along the front and sides, embellished the second story. Aged, yet still graceful, columns supported the whole length, lending a stately, if weathered, elegance to the late nineteenth century structure. She loved old buildings and the heritage they represented. Fortunately, Cord shared her love of the old. A surprisingly large amount of his work was in restoring these former showplaces. It was her job to see that the grounds matched the buildings' history like an invisible cloak. Cord believed a building without the proper setting was like the Hope Diamond set in tinfoil. In so many ways she and Cord were so alike.

"Places like this always get to me, too."

Startled, Victoria whirled around to find Thorn Jansen smiling at her. "I didn't realize you'd arrived already," she murmured after only the briefest of hesitations.

Thorn Jansen simply smiled before returning his attention to the house his aunt had left him. A frown chased the pleasure from his face. "It isn't in very good shape. The outside is riddled with rotten boards. I hope Darcourte can turn the place back into the beauty it was in its prime." He pointed to the railing on the balcony. "Most of those vertical pieces will need replacement. And with that carved design, it's going to take extra time." He turned back to Victoria. "That's just the outside. I really want to get this finished for my wife's birthday. She lived down the road from here and always loved this old place. She wanted to raise our children here, but we couldn't have afforded the place then, even if my aunt had been willing to sell it."

Victoria listened carefully to more than the words. It was important to know her clients as people in order to create settings that would match their personalities and life-styles. She liked the Jansen couple. Married for over thirty years, they were a living example of the commitment and love possible in a marriage.

"The inside is worse." Thorn waved a hand encompassing the whole neglected property. "Maybe I should have planned my surprise for next year rather than this one."

Victoria shook her head. He had already told her how important the birthday coming up was to him and his wife. If there was any way humanly possible, she wanted his home to be finished for the red-letter day.

"If Cord said we could get it ready in time, then that's what we'll do," Victoria stated positively.

He searched her face before he gave a decisive nod. "You two think a lot of each other, don't you? Did your partner tell you that I had another firm in mind for landscaping and that he told me it was either a package deal or nothing?"

Victoria stared at him, not doubting his statement for a moment. It was just the sort of thing Cord would do. "No, he didn't." She spread her hands awkwardly. "What can I say?"

"Nothing. He has probably already said enough for all of us. He said you would work a miracle with the grounds." He glanced around and then back at her. "I think it will take at least that to make this place beautiful again."

Privately, Victoria agreed with him. "Cord is good at working miracles."

Four

Victoria left the restaurant after an extra long lunch-break. Once she had finished at the Jansen site, she hadn't been eager to face Cord again. So she had taken her time driving back to town and, on impulse, decided to treat herself to a leisurely meal. With that done, she couldn't put off returning any longer.

Maybelle was on the phone when she entered. Victoria had gotten to her desk when the import of what Maybelle was saying made itself felt. Maybelle was canceling Cord's appointments. She stopped, staring a little.

"What's going on?" she asked as soon as Maybelle hung up.

"Don't know. Cord came roaring out of his office a half hour ago and told me to clear his schedule. I know he was trying to find you earlier." She frowned, looking puzzled and worried at the same time. "What's with him lately? I'm used to his tempers, in fact I'd miss them if they suddenly stopped, but he's been a grouch even for him. He acts as though he's worried about something. Do you know what's wrong?"

Victoria shook her head. "No. But, if it makes you feel any better, I'm wondering too. Did he say where he was going or when he would be back?"

"No, and that's not like him, either. He always tells us where he'll be." The phone rang. Maybelle grimaced as she answered.

Victoria walked down the hall. Speculating about Cord's behavior was worse than useless. If he had wanted them to know what he was up to, he would have told them. She tried to console herself with the knowledge that there was very little he couldn't handle. She spent the rest of the afternoon working and listening for his return. Her worry increased when he didn't. Finally, she could put off going home no longer.

Once she reached her apartment she tried to unwind. It had been a long tiring day but she couldn't relax. She was too restless. Suddenly the doorbell rang. She wasn't expecting anyone. Cord stood in the hall as she opened the door.

"May I come in?" he asked quietly.

"Yes." She stepped back, watching him and trying to conceal that she was. Cord breezed, stalked or stomped, depending on his mood. He never walked in and politely waited for her to take a seat. The unprecedented behavior wasn't reassuring.

"We have to talk."

"I thought we had." She didn't like the determination in his voice or the deep gravity. Uneasy, wary, she attempted to act casual. She couldn't forget the words they had spoken.

Sighing, Cord shook his head. "You know we haven't. At least not enough so that we don't avoid each other if we can. I waited for you this morning. It didn't take me long to figure out you were prolonging your time out of the office. That kind of thing will affect your work."

Victoria lifted her chin, irritated at having been caught out. "I know very well it will affect my work in the long run. Today was a special case and you know it."

He held on to his temper. It had taken him most of the afternoon to decide to confront her. He wasn't about to let her temper push his own. Then neither of them would get anywhere.

"I've been giving our situation a lot of thought." Why hadn't he realized how difficult this would be? "I don't want to spend my day really fighting with you. I don't want you feeling you have to avoid me. Whatever is going on between us needs to be resolved."

He had opened the door, but she couldn't step through. She couldn't just say, *I want you.* "I don't know what you're talking about beyond your unreasoning jealousy," she replied finally, when it was clear he would wait until Armageddon arrived for an answer.

"What about yours?"

She drew back, not expecting the accusation. "I don't know—"

He stopped her with a sharp, too perceptive look. "Don't lie."

She got to her feet to pace the room. "All right, I admit it. I don't think Darlene is good enough for you in much the same way you think James would have hurt me if I had been interested in him. We're friends, you and I. Why shouldn't I be concerned with who you see and how you are doing? Is it so impossible to believe that I want you to be happy?"

Cord tried not to be affected by her words. He didn't want to feel good because she cared about who he saw. He wanted the time back when they were friends, but each went their separate ways. He understood that relationship. Needing something to do with his hands, he reached into his pocket and took out a stick of gum. "So it's just your concern for me?" He watched her lie and didn't call her on it.

"Yes."

He clenched his jaws and silently damned his honor to hell and back. If Victoria hadn't been his friend, if they hadn't shared so much, including their partnership, he could have worked her out of his system with a wild and exciting affair. Then they could have parted and his life would have been back on track. As things stood, that course was impossible. He had a sneaking feeling that if he took Victoria to bed nothing would ever be the same again. But was their current situation any better? His emotions were out of control. His mind at constant war with his body. He couldn't sleep for dreaming of her. Work was an irritant. His life was erupting, shaking the earth beneath his feet. Something had to give. For the first time ever he was prepared to compromise.

"And if I tell you that there is nothing going on between us, and that there won't be, then everything should be square between us?" He slouched in his seat, looking at her.

She was weary and mussed from a long day and she was still the most beautiful woman he knew. He wanted to slide his fingers into her hair, massage away the headache the faint furrow between her brows indicated. The thought and the need irritated him.

"I don't see why not." She tried a shrug and was vaguely pleased when she pulled it off without feeling stiff.

"Good. Then come out with me to dinner tomorrow night. We'll talk and relax. You need a break and so do I." He was taking a chance. Maybe if he spent time with her as a woman, he could find the friend. It was a long shot and not even logical, but he had to try something before he lost her completely.

She froze, her eyes going to his face, searching his expression. The blandness of it warned her to tread carefully. "Why?"

"Why not? Afraid?"

"Of what?"

"Me?" He got to his feet, watching her back away until she came up against the wall. All the promises he had made to himself about how to come to terms with his desire for her went up in smoke. He couldn't see her without wondering what she would feel like in his arms, responding to him as a man. He should walk away, but even that was beyond him.

"I'm afraid of no man." Her chin came up. She had spent too much effort learning how to handle herself in whatever situation Fate threw at her. Be it man, beast, or Cord, she would survive.

"Good." His head bent. He had been thinking about her mouth, the way she would taste, too long to deny himself now. His hands settled on her shoulders, ready to support or hold, depending on her reaction.

"Cord?" She watched his eyes, seeing a depth she had never known. Desire burned there. A steady heat penetrated her suit, bringing the scent of his body to tease her senses. His lips brushed hers, lightly. She froze, caught in the trap of sensations she couldn't control. When his mouth settled on hers, she sighed. Immediately he took advantage of the breath to touch her tongue with his. Gently, he stroked the moist length, turning the act into an erotic game she had never experienced. His body pressed her against the wall, making her aware of his strength and his arousal. Her hips tipped, cradling him. Heat surged in her, rhythmic pulses urging her to push against him, then retreat. He groaned against her throat, fighting for breath and a measure of restraint. The second cost him most of the first.

"Do you know what you're doing?" He lifted his head to gaze into her eyes. The dazed look told a story too eloquent to be denied. He hadn't expected her response. Part of him wanted to shout at her to stop him. "Is this what you want?" he asked, his hand slipping down her throat to settle on her breast.

The thin silk teased rather than hid the tiny nub that poked against his palm. His fingers flicked the nipple and she moaned, her head falling back over his arms. He lifted her against him. He hadn't meant to do more than give her a taste of what could be theirs. Now he couldn't stop. It would be too easy to carry her to the couch or to her bedroom. She was soft in his arms, all woman and wanting him.

"I want you," he whispered, taking her lips again. "Come home with me. We can be good together."

Want. The one word she couldn't ignore. Want was not need, nor was it love. Either, she could have handled. But not this. He offered her what he gave to the other women in his life. She wanted more than that.

"Let me go," she said, fighting herself and him with words. "I don't want this."

"Your body says you do." His hand stroked lightly down her breast to settle on her abdomen.

Victoria couldn't stop the involuntary arch of her hips against the heavy weight. "It won't work. I won't be your latest bedmate." She tried to push out of his arms. He held her fast, looking down at her. "I won't be like Darlene."

"You couldn't be if you tried."

"Let me go." She didn't know if he was complimenting her or not. She didn't want to give in to the need to ask.

Cord frowned, then released her. "Why are you afraid?"

"Stop saying that." She turned away, needing to put some distance between them. Her fingers went to her temple, massaging lightly. "We're friends. Our relationship is important to me and now you're trying to change it, trying to turn me into something I'm not."

Cord sighed, closing his eyes for a moment. Patience had never been his strong point. He shouldn't have rushed her. Now he had to convince her to relax.

"Maybe I'm rushing you. I don't think so, but you do. Come out with me. Call it a meal like the others we've shared if it makes you feel better."

Victoria glanced over her shoulder. "You're up to something."

"What could I be up to?"

She shook her head, puzzled, lost and aching with unfulfilled needs. She wanted to be with him.

"Say yes." He walked toward her, ready to stop the moment she showed signs of retreating. He lowered his head slowly, watching her watching him. Her eyes were large, curious as he brushed her lips. The sweet taste of her breath mingling with his stirred the sleeping demon of desire. He caged the animal and tried for tenderness. "Come out with me tomorrow."

Victoria was caught by the tenderness. Temper she could handle, but his gentleness undid her. Her fingers slipped from his grasp to touch his cheek. "I'm afraid. I might lose you." Fear drove the words out of her. "You've been in my life for so long. All that I have now, I owe to you. I couldn't bear not having you as a friend."

"Damn that word! Don't call me that anymore. And don't give me gratitude either. I never wanted it. Not from you, not from—" He jerked away from her. "Forget it. This isn't going to work. I was a fool. I know it." He headed for the door.

Victoria grabbed his arm. Her temper was as hair-trigger as his own. Emotion lent strength to her slim body. Setting her heels, she jerked him around to face her. "You started this, you big lug. You asked me out. You kissed me. Remember? Now I'm accepting. I told you what I was thinking because we have never been

less than honest with one another. So don't act like
more than a fool than you can help. I'll be ready by
seven and you better be here to pick me up. I hate
being stood up. It will put me in a mood that will make
all of your tantrums seem like tales from *Mary Pop-
pins*," she warned. She didn't know why he had blown
up, and right now she was in no mood to care.

Cord looked down at her flushed face, wishing he
had the nerve to swing her into his arms, forget the
dating bit, and head straight for bed. She'd skin him
with a dull knife if he tried, so he opted for the next-
best thing. One arm snaked out and hauled her to him.
His mouth covered hers before she could object. The
kiss branded them both. He was breathing as hard as
she when he released her. He wasn't sure where he got
the energy for a grin.

"See you at seven tomorrow night, honey." He got
out of the apartment before she could recover. He
wanted to keep his head where it was. The thud of
something heavy hitting the floor told him he had escaped just in time. Victoria did not like being outma-
neuvered.

Victoria let him leave, knowing she was a fool for
even considering going. "Justifiably, certifiably in-
sane," she muttered.

But maybe she wasn't. She stopped in the middle of
the hall, a shocked look on her face. Maybe this was
her chance to get some answers. Perhaps she did need
to go out with him. Wasn't it time she understood the
demons that seemed to drive him? Maybe understanding would give her a way to get herself and her
emotions back on track. Maybe it was time to ask
questions, demand answers.

Five

Victoria awoke with the sun and lay considering the evening ahead. She hadn't slept well but right now that didn't matter. She had to think, to plan. She wouldn't put it past Cord to have played out the whole scenario the night before just to get the date he wanted. She'd murder him if she discovered he had tricked her. There wouldn't be one place in the whole city where he could hide.

A date! He had given her the opening. She was a fool not to use it to her advantage if she could. She wanted more from Cord than his body. That was becoming more apparent with each passing day. After seven tonight he would never again see her as the woman he had to protect and help through life. A definitely less-than-nice intent was a wonderful antidote for almost no sleep. Victoria made breakfast, knowing she would need the energy before the day was over. She was going shopping.

Armor hunting might have been a more apt description for her plans. Not just any dress would do. She wanted something that Cord had not seen and, more importantly, something that would curl his eyelashes, fry his socks and dispel forever the word "friend" from both their vocabularies. Eight stores later she found the gown.

White. The color was the first and the last virginal thing about it. The bodice started at one shoulder, gathered in tiny silk pleats across her breast, molding to every curve. What there was of the back began and ended at her waist. The skirt skimmed her knees to slide up a side slit that stopped just barely at the point of modesty. Victoria surveyed herself in the mirror and decided Darlene would have approved. No man in a ten-mile radius would be able to ignore this dress. The very lack of ornamentation drew the eye to the wearer.

"Madame, the dress is made for you. Whoever is your man, he is going to find you too beautiful to resist." The saleswoman smiled, a world of knowledge in the dark eyes that studied Victoria. "A dress to kill."

Victoria laughed softly. "With any luck at all," she agreed. "Now all I need is the accessories."

The other woman clicked her fingers. "I have just the thing. I'll be right back." She slipped through the curtain to return a minute later with a fluff of white thrown over one arm and a glitter of silver and crystal in the other hand. "Try these. They just came in today. I haven't had a chance to put them on display."

Victoria studied the effect in the mirror. She would definitely get Cord's attention now.

"They look as if they were made for this dress." Victoria took the fluff. It was a shawl of delicate lace, so fine that it looked like silver-shot cobwebs. The light fabric settled on her shoulders, adding a touch of mystery, cloaking the revealing dress with teasing shadows. The glitter was a single bracelet meant to be worn as a slave-girl ornament above the elbow. The result was a pagan look that suited Victoria both emotionally and physically.

The saleswoman smiled widely, delighted at the creation. "I'm glad you like it. Not many women could wear this outfit," she admitted. "Whoever this guy is, he doesn't stand a chance."

Victoria laughed softly, looking at her reflection. "That's the general idea." For one moment she savored the thought of the look on Cord's face. Then her own clouded with doubt. In her desire to wreak havoc, she had forgotten the consequences of the course she had chosen. "But maybe it is too much," she murmured to herself.

The other woman shook her head. "It's in perfect taste."

Victoria knew the saleswoman was right but she needed the reassurance. "I think I'm having an attack of nerves. Pay no attention. I'll take the dress and the rest of these lovely things."

She beamed. "I am so glad. I have loved this dress since I saw it at the spring show. Until now I have thought no one could do it justice. I will leave you now to change." She whisked herself away before Victoria could change her mind.

Victoria left the shop with her purchases under her arm. Despite the fact the shoes were easy to find, there was little of the afternoon left. She spent most of it doing her weekend chores. She didn't want to think, so she didn't. She wasn't sure what she wanted from Cord anymore. He had changed the picture she carried of him. And in changing his, her own was also altered.

Cord stared out his apartment window. Lunch was hours ago, not that he had eaten much. He had work in the den he should be doing. Jansen's plans still weren't complete. Yet here he sat, thinking of Victoria.

Gratitude! He hated the emotion. It crippled all it touched, creating envy and jealousy where there should be love. It tied and trapped where there should be only freedom. It enslaved both the giver and the taker. It destroyed, damaged. Was he destined to spend his life fighting those who would feel grateful to him?

He glared at the view that normally pleased him. Maybe he should have left well enough alone, but he had come too far to go back now. His desire was no longer something he could control, something he no longer wanted to control. Victoria wasn't indifferent to him. He could build on that, creating pleasure for her and himself for a time. It wouldn't last; nothing ever did. But he would have those moments.

What if they could not go back to a friendship once the loving was done? The doubt struck deep. He fought it down.

What if! His life had been filled too often with those two words. Regrets, chances not taken, courses chosen that failed for reasons he had been too blind to see. Secrets. He hated them too. He had them, too many. He kept them because he dared not share them. If he showed Victoria the man, would she sense the dark areas of his life? Would she demand to know what hid in the shadows?

He knew that need drove him. He had fought it for so long until he could fight no longer. He would try. He would keep his secrets. He would give what he could if she would let him, but he would keep his secrets out of necessity. Rising from the chair, he headed for his room. It was time to get ready. She had decreed seven. For the first time since he had left her he smiled.

It would be almost worth it to keep her waiting just to see what she would do.

Victoria twisted this way and that. The reflection in her mirror was even more explicit than the one in the store dressing room. There was definitely too little of the gown. She had meant to tempt Cord a little, not incinerate him. Groaning at her own stupidity and impulsiveness, Victoria started to unzip the dress. The doorbell rang before she could finish. It was too late.

She hadn't been this nervous at her own wedding, Victoria realized. She left her room slowly, putting off the moment as long as possible. Another impatient knock sounded. She opened the door, stepping back. She forgot the dress as she stared at Cord. She missed the flash of desire in his eyes.

He was handsome! His jacket fit smoothly over his broad shoulders, his dark slacks outlined long legs. His features bore the stamp of his personality, intense, intelligent and vibrantly alive. It was hard to believe she had known him for so long without being aware of him.

"You're beautiful," Cord said quietly, seeing the dazed look in her eyes. He moved forward, drawing her into his arms as he pushed the door shut with his foot. "I should have known you'd play with fire."

Victoria went to him. She wanted to touch him, to feel his arms around her. "I shouldn't have bought it," she whispered. "I'm not even certain now why I did."

"Right now I don't care why. I like it, but more than that, I like you in it." He bent his head to touch her lips. He teased them, brushing lightly across the full contours, hearing her breath catch in her throat at his caress. Desire rippled through him. His fingers tightened on her waist.

Victoria leaned into him, her hands sliding up to his shoulders. "We should stop. We'll regret this in a minute."

"No."

"This is madness."

"Divine madness." His tongue flicked out to lick the corners of her mouth. Her lips opened in a silent plea he ignored for he wanted to savor the intimacy for as long as possible. If he really kissed her, he would want too much. He traced the line of her jaw to her ear. A nip on the lobe had her shivering in his arms. "You like that, honey."

"Stop teasing and kiss me." The words were a demand, the tone pleading.

He smiled as he lifted his head. "I've waited a long time for you to be in my arms. I'm not rushing one second of this." He urged her closer until her hips fit into the cradle of his. "See how much I want you." He glanced down at the thin silk that covered her breasts. "See how much you want me."

Victoria followed his gaze, her eyes wide at the sight of her nipples outlined in white. The hard tips seemed to be straining for Cord's chest as though they sought the warmth that waited there. She inhaled deeply and they inched closer.

"Before the night is over I'll see them. You'll undress for me."

The words poured over her, stealing the strength from her legs. She clung to him as she raised her head. "Cord?"

Finally, the desire he had waited to see smoldered in her eyes. "What do you want?"

"Kiss me, please."

"And the rest?"

"Now!"

He shook his head. "Later." The disappointment in her expression pleased him as nothing had in a long time. Her reward and his was the kiss they both needed. Her lips met his halfway. Hers was no ladylike gesture. His held no tenderness. They burned too much. The need was stronger than the gentler feelings both possessed. Victoria's breath emerged on a ragged sigh as Cord broke the kiss.

"No. More!"

Cord heard the frustration, understanding it more than she could know. He was on the outer edge of his control. Only the knowledge of what he could lose if he rushed them kept him sane. He pulled her closer, needing the ache of holding her tight against his body to assuage the desire writhing within.

Victoria fought him then. She could feel him withdrawing from her. She tried to free her arms, but he guessed her intent.

"No. Stay. Let me help us both." His hands smoothed over her bare back, easing the quivers of passion that raced over her skin. "It hurts now, but it will go away. Wait."

"Why, Cord? Why do this to either of us?"

"I had to know."

She stared at him, trying to understand. Nothing made sense. He had brought her to the fever pitch of wanting and hadn't taken what she would have gladly given. If she had known him less, she would have accused him of taunting her with his power, his experience.

"I don't understand."

He smiled slightly, although it took an effort. "You will, I promise." She was relaxing in his arms. The desire was loosening its grip. The weight of her lying against him was a pleasure he could not have explained if asked. "Better now?"

She nodded. "How did you know it would help?" When his brow cocked in question, she added, "The holding?"

He chuckled softly. "You don't want to know." He knew his answer would prod her temper.

Victoria's eyes flickered with irritation. She pushed out of his arms. "You could have lied, blast you, Cordell Jackson—"

He leaned forward to kiss the rest of his name from her lips. She was nearly dancing with outrage at his tactics when he lifted his head. He laughed, feeling good. He caught both her hands. His safety could easily be at risk if the look in her eyes was anything to go by. He lifted them to his lips. "Come on, I have reservations at your favorite restaurant, and we don't want to be late."

"I've just changed my mind. I don't want to go anywhere with you," Victoria stated, lying and not caring. His disbelieving look sent her temper up a notch. "I don't like being manipulated."

Cord ignored the charge. He drew her toward the couch, where he could see a shawl and handbag lay. Tucking both hands in one of his, he draped the covering over her shoulders and slipped her purse into his coat pocket. "Have you got everything?"

Victoria planted her feet. "I will not be moved around as if I were a doll," she said, glaring at him.

"Do you want me to carry you? I can you know. Of course, it is a ways to the car. The easiest method would be for me to toss you over my shoulder." He waited, enjoying her in a way he couldn't explain. So much of what he felt for and about Victoria was incomprehensible to him. He just knew he wanted her fiery disposition almost as much as he wanted the woman. When he denied himself one, he stirred the other.

"You wouldn't dare!" His look said he would. She swallowed, torn between anger and the intrigue of being carried off like a prize. What woman could re-sist the man who could make her feel so desirable and so helpless at one and the same time? "I'll get you for this," she promised. He couldn't have everything his own way.

"I know. I can't wait."

Six

———

Are you going to sulk the whole evening?'' Cord glanced at Victoria's profile, smiling a little in the darkness. She hadn't said a word since they had gotten into his car. He knew she wasn't sulking. Victoria never held a grudge or used emotions to get her own way. Everything about her was honest and straightforward.

"I'm thinking," she replied after a moment. "It just occurred to me how often you make me angry enough to feel like hitting you. No one else, just you. Do you do it on purpose?"

His grin widened. Her mind fascinated him. It always had. "What do you think?" He wouldn't make it easy for her.

"I think you do."

"And?"

Victoria glanced at him. This time his amusement didn't prod her temper. She was on the right track and nothing he did would get her off it until she had some answers. She had to understand him. So often Cord, a master at evasion, slipped away from her.

"I think you use my temper and yours to keep us out of deep water," she stated, watching him closely. His quick look told her more than his carefully blank expression. Just for a moment she wished she had chosen a better place for this discussion. The street-lights weren't bright enough to read his face.

Cord didn't like the direction of her thoughts. "What brought me into the conversation? I thought we were talking about you."

"I won't be sidetracked."

"Is that what you think I'm doing?"

"And answering a question with a question won't work, either." The more he sidestepped, the more determined she became.

"Will reaching our destination?"

"It will postpone it. That's all." She turned more fully in her seat, reaching out to lay her hand on his arm. "I need to understand you. Do you realize I know next to nothing about you? Do you have any family? Where were you born? Where did you go to school? Ordinary things. Your past is like one great blank screen. Why? You know so much about me. Is it that you can't trust me?" It hurt more than she would have believed possible to ask the last question.

Cord caught her hand. "I do trust you," he said roughly. "It's just that my past isn't important to me. It never has been. I live in the present, you know that." That was the first lie he had ever told her.

"Are you sure?" Victoria searched his expression, sensing more than just secrets in his manner. Perhaps she had no right to ask. Perhaps friendship, and whatever else they were building between them, didn't allow for her digging into his history. Yet wasn't it natural that she should be curious? Did he really expect her to pretend his life began with adulthood?

"I'm sure." He glanced away from her dark eyes. "Shall we go in before they give our table away?"

Victoria frowned briefly at the light question. Her unease deepened. She couldn't put her finger on what was wrong. Images of the times he had given her space to think, to keep her thoughts to herself, rose up to taunt her. He had a right to find his own time to confide in her, if he ever did.

"I'm starved," she said, making herself smile. Inside she was a confusion of emotion. Cord was so much more than she had ever seen. The need to understand him completely was growing by the second. Friendship was slipping into a new guise, stronger, more demanding, more intense.

Cord looked back at her, relaxing at the faint smile she gave him. The crisis was over. "Then let's eat." He got out of the car, keeping hold of her hand. She had to slide across the seat to join him. "I do like that dress," he teased as she got out to stand beside him.

She laughed, knowing full well the skimpy bodice had given him a peek at her breasts. With any other man, she would have been embarrassed. With Cord, she felt delighted that he wanted her enough to look.

"You're a lecher, Cord."

He tucked her arm through his. "Sometimes," he agreed, amusement in his voice. "But not nearly as much as I used to be."

Victoria shot him a look. Cord cryptic was Cord serious. "Does that mean that you've ceased to roam the halls of the bachelor?"

Did the earth grow silent or was it her imagination, she wondered, as she waited for Cord to answer. It wasn't in her to become the latest in the select string of beautiful women who had graced his bed. She needed more than that. Not necessarily marriage—God knows she had learned that that institution was vastly over-rated—or even a formal commitment, but more than just weeks or months of mutual pleasure. Perhaps Cord had taught her too well. In her youth and inexperience she had let George mold her into someone who didn't exist. Cord had taught her to value herself.

Cord stopped and pulled her into the shadows lining the walk. A magnolia tree shaded them from the view of incoming guests. "If you are asking if there will be another woman, the answer is no. It's you I want. No one else."

"For how long?" She whispered the words, almost afraid to say them aloud.

He caught her shoulders, molding her to him. "For as long as the wanting exists. For as long as the sun shines and we're glad we're together. For as long as it takes."

Fear rippled through her. "That sounds like forever. I don't want promises from you. Don't give me pretty words because you think I need them. You told me once you would never marry, that you would never

commit yourself to one woman. You meant it then. I
know it.'' The words tumbled out. Her emotions were
too close to the surface to allow for discretion. ''And
I'm not even sure anymore that I could be with a man
that way. George hurt me badly.''

Cord gazed into her eyes and saw the panic. She
would live in the present as he always had. He should
have been happy she wanted no ties, he should have
taken exactly what she offered and given her his passion.

She didn't want to hurt his feelings, but she couldn't
lie either. ''You have always tried to help me—''

''I won't be responsible if this is going to be one of
those gratitude speeches you lay on me when the mood
strikes you,'' he said roughly. Would she never learn?

''But don't you see, you're still trying to protect
me?''

''Is that what you think I'm doing?'' He laughed
humorlessly. Releasing her, he reached into his pocket
for his cigarettes. He swore when he remembered he
was quitting. He glanced at his watch, then at the entrance to the restaurant. ''We're going to be late. Let's
go.'' He gestured toward the walk but didn't touch her.

Victoria frowned, wondering at the brooding quality of his voice and expression. ''What's wrong? Tell
me so that I can understand,'' she begged when he
made no move to touch her.

''What could be wrong?'' Cord gave her a sharp
glance.

The worried expression in her eyes made him angry. Nothing was going as he had expected. In many
ways he and Victoria were so close. They had eaten
together many times, laughing and talking as only

truly compatible people can. Now he found he could think of little to say. Even after they were seated at the table overlooking the gardens, conversation lagged. Vintage wine, soft music, good food. Nothing helped. He tried and so did she. Their sentences were stilted, awkward. The pauses too long. Neither allowed their eyes to linger on the other.

After their meal Cord drove home, regretting much of his actions. Regret was something he seldom allowed himself to feel, having learned the futility of the emotion from bitter experience.

"I'd rather you didn't come in," Victoria said quietly, when Cord parked the car and started to get out.

He froze, half-turned away from her. Frustration almost spilled out in a torrent of words. He bit them back. He had already said too much, pushed too fast. He turned slowly to watch her. She was nervous. Her hands were clasped tightly in her lap, her eyes flickering between him and the building before them.

"We need to talk."

"We tried that. It didn't work."

"So we try again."

She shook her head. "Maybe we're just meant to be friends. Tonight was a mess for both of us. Not your fault and not mine. It just was. I don't want us to do this again. I need to be able to laugh with you and talk about things that matter to us." She leaned forward to lay her hand on his arm. "I don't care about the weather, the color scheme of the redecorating we're going to do in the office, or if you should trade your car. Those things have a place, but not as a filler for silences neither of us can tolerate."

"What do you want? To pretend I never kissed you?"

Cornered, she replied with the unvarnished truth. "Yes! Yes! We made a mistake. Both of us. Me, because it is time I started dating; and you, because you're trying to help."

Cord clenched his jaws, imprisoning the denials screaming for release. How could one woman be so blind! "All right! You win!" he snapped, too angry to care if he was shouting. "Go back to your chaste little bed. I won't bother you again. I'll pretend you don't twist my stomach in knots every time you walk in the room. I'll sit back and watch you go out with some fool. But this time I won't be around to pick up the pieces. I'm no masochist. I've waited as long as I'm going to wait for you."

Victoria gathered her handbag and slipped from the car. She walked quickly away, refusing to look back, although the need tore at her. She had told him the truth. So why was she crying, she asked herself as his car roared into the night. The angry sound of the engine, the squeal of the tires, emphasized the words Cord had thrown at her. She entered her apartment without turning on the light. She didn't want to see herself in the mirror. She didn't want to see she was alone. She dropped limply onto the bed, wishing she understood what had happened to the evening that had begun with so much promise.

Cord wanted her. She wanted him. She had known she couldn't handle being just one in a string of Cord's women, but she hadn't expected him to offer her much more than that. Her own demons about trusting a man to stay with her had been forgotten until Cord had spoken of staying together. Panic, unexpected and too strong to hide, had torn them apart. She and Cord were a pair, both caught in a past neither seemed able to change. She felt the fool, blowing first hot then cold. Cord had every right to be angry.

And that anger dried her tears. She got off the bed in one swift surge and went to the closet. One of them had to be willing to give in. Knowing Cord and how he considered her needs before his own, it wouldn't be him. Yanking off the dress she had spent so much time buying, she pulled on a pair of jeans and a Western-cut shirt. She'd bet even now Cord was on his way to the house on the bayou. He never spent the weekend in town unless he had work to do.

In less than an hour she was on the road. He might throw her out, might even think she had lost her mind, but she was going to him. A smile trembled on her lips then firmed into a grin. If he took her in, she knew he'd never let her forget she had come to him. Her only retaliation lay in reminding him how chicken-hearted he had been in giving up. She wouldn't tell him how much she had needed time to think things through. The grin died to be replaced by a thoughtful frown. On second thought, she might just kill him. It would be just like him to maneuver her into making the first move. He knew how badly George had marked her. He might just be trying to let her find her feet with a good healthy push from behind by him.

She parked her car in his driveway, glaring at the neat way his Porsche was parked ahead of her. Cord hadn't been in much of a temper, after all, if he could take time to be so precise when there was such a huge area to use. She stomped up the steps and entered without knocking.

Cord looked up from pouring her a glass of wine. "You took your own sweet time getting here," he stated, coming toward her. He offered her the glass he held, wondering if she would toss it back in his face. She was fully capable of the action. He hadn't been as sure as he wanted her to think, nor had he planned on spilling his thoughts earlier in a burst of anger.

"You are without a doubt the most devious, most low-down, conniving male I have had the misfortune to know." Victoria stabbed a finger in his chest. "You planned this, you rat. For two cents I'd go right back to town and leave you out here."

He hadn't planned anything, but he wasn't about to admit it. Reaching into his pocket, he offered her two pennies. Once he had cooled down, he hadn't been sure he hadn't blown his chances completely. With all that had gone between them, it hadn't occurred to him that she wouldn't be able to trust herself to a relationship with him. He had honestly thought the only hurdles he had to overcome were the ties of their friendship.

Victoria stared at him, then at the money he held in the palm of his hand. "Talk about the lady-or-the-tiger dilemma," Victoria muttered.

"I want you to want me for myself. Is that so difficult to understand?" He watched her intently. Even now he wasn't sure which she would choose.

"There are times, Cord Darcourte, when I don't like the way you understand me," she said, snatching the glass of wine out of his hand. A little sloshed over onto his fingers.

Cord grinned at her temper, more relieved than he would admit even to himself. He lifted his fingers to his mouth to lick the wine from his skin as he pocketed the money. His eyes held hers, reading the passion that smoldered under all the other emotions.

"Kiss me, woman." He pulled her to him, needing the feel of her body against his. She was real and she was finally here.

Victoria came to him, torn between yelling at him and giving into the desire growing stronger within her by the second. "I ought to pour this all over you."

"But you won't." He smiled at her.

Her eyes narrowed on that grin. "You're treading on thin ice."

He bent his head and took her lips. He had denied himself long enough.

The first touch was so light, so gentle, that Victoria froze, suspended in time. Her anger slipped from her grasp. She had expected the drive of his emotion, the need in him. Instead she found tantalizing touches. When her breath came in through parted lips, it brought with it the subtle taste of Cord. He kissed the corners of her mouth, outlining the curve of her lips with the moist tip of his tongue, and then brushed his mouth repeatedly over hers. Each gliding caress seemed to have no ending or beginning.

Deep inside her body, Victoria felt herself come apart with a slow liquid unraveling that brought a soft moan to her throat.

"Victoria? What is it?" Cord sensed something was happening, something beautiful, and he wanted to be a part of it in the fullest way possible.

It was almost impossible to open her eyes. "You make me feel so beautiful. George never made me feel like this. And it was only a kiss." The wonder she felt was in her voice.

It was reflected in his eyes as he stared at the woman in his arms. The words both humbled and exalted Cord, shaking him with a fierce pleasure he had never known until this moment. "Thank you," he said huskily. Then he whispered against Victoria's throat, "Touching you is more than I dreamed it would be."

Victoria shivered as Cord's lips found the sensitive rim of her ear. The tip of his tongue spiraled lightly down and in, until he knew all the secret whorls. For a moment the tip hardened, probing then retreating, giving and taking warmth with each thrust. Victoria trembled and made a small sound. Cord lifted his head and looked at her through half-closed eyes, reading the pleasure and the growing passion in the tension in her body. His hand shaped her neck, savoring the soft flesh and the throb of life beneath his thumb.

Victoria reached out to Cord, her fingers seeking his warmth. Somehow the glass of wine he had given her was gone. Nothing separated them but the air they breathed and the clothes they wore.

"I ache, Cord," she confessed in a rush, nuzzling her face into the soft hair framed by the open shirt-front. Her mouth rubbed against his skin, tasting him, inhaling the scent of him. "I want you." She raised her head, her eyes heavy with desire.

"I'm glad, because I want you too." Cord bent and lifted her to his chest. He carried her to the den and the fluffy rug that lay before the fire burning in the hearth. He lowered her to the mat, coming down beside her to lie half across her. He needed to feel her beneath him, accepting him as though she had known only his touch.

Tremors raced through Victoria, echoing deep in his body. Blood pooled hotly until his control was stretched to the edges of restraint. His fingers freed the buttons of her shirt. He had to touch her. Her hands on his back tightened, urging him closer in silent invitations. He took her mouth, his tongue answering her thrusts with increasing hunger. His lips moved down the taut line of her throat. Head back, eyes closed, Victoria abandoned herself to the delicious sensation of Cord's caresses. His mouth drifted over the curve of her breast, then closed with melting gentleness over her nipple. Victoria shivered and arched into his touch, glorying in the pleasure he gave her. His teeth raked lightly over the nipple.

Her moan ripped through Cord, pain and pleasure combined. Her shirt was in the way. He pulled it free, no longer able to give her tenderness. Her jeans followed with her help. His shirt and pants were discarded by Victoria's trembling hands. She looked into his eyes when they lay naked together. Then she gave him a gift he had not expected.

A long slow smile. Eve herself could not have tempted Adam so well.

"Witch woman," he whispered as he rose above her. His hips moved against her, telling her exactly how much he needed her. She quivered in his arms, twisting beneath him wildly. Running the sensitive soles of her feet up and down his flexed calves, trying to capture him inside her. His hand stroked down her body and found the liquid heat of her, a single touch that sent tiny, passionate convulsions rippling through her body.

"Now, Cord," she pleaded.

Cord took her mouth and her body in one smooth motion, becoming a part of her. She melted around him until two became one. He moved with care, wanting the first time to be more special than anything he had ever done before. He fit her perfectly, hot and snug, caressing her even when he was still. She smiled again and murmured words that had no meaning, simply sounds telling him of her pleasure.

He moved slowly, savoring every motion of their bodies. He wanted this moment to last forever. Victoria writhed, needing his weight, needing more than care. She needed passion, hard driving, aching, fulfilling passion. Her hands tightened.

"More." Her demand was a plea.

Her hungry seeking took Cord's breath away. Instinctively he gave her what she wanted, holding nothing back. With each speeding motion, each instant of shaking pleasure, he knew he should hold back slightly, not take the chance of hurting her. Then he felt the intimate pulses of her release all around him and it was too late for anything but the desire he had denied for so long. His body arched into her, tearing a cry of ecstasy from their lips at the same time. He shuddered and arched again and again, giving himself to her as deeply as she had given of herself to him.

For long, sweet minutes Victoria and Cord lay spent in each other's arms, drifting slowly back to an awareness of the quiet room, the fire burning in the hearth and the feel of the rug beneath her body. Victoria looked at Cord, the taste of him still on her lips, the feel of his body joined with hers still a reality. Her fingers moved down his back to the tight muscles of his buttocks and beyond, tracing his shadowed curves the way he had traced hers earlier. Cord groaned and tightened inside her, sending sensations streaking through her. She was so sensitive to him that arousal was only a breath away. She caressed him again, learning his contours in a way she had done with no man.

"Victoria," Cord whispered, his low voice both husky and amused. "Do you know what you're doing?" He wanted her even now, when their bodies were still slick with the dew of their passion.

He moved deeply inside her, stealing her answer. He drank her cry of need as one who thirsted in the desert. "Is this what you want?"

Cord saw the surprise in Victoria's eyes, felt it in the clinging of her body as she sought to increase the closeness between them. Passion tightened in Cord, hunger uncoiling to touch every part of his being. The claws of desire were blunted but not without points. He felt each one as a separate ache he had to ease. And only Victoria held the power to cage the beast within.

"Cord?" Victoria panted, her breath shortening with each stroke of his body. "Is it possible?"

He laughed, glorying in the force that drove them both. "Do you doubt it, witch?" he demanded, his voice thick with a man's wanting. "I told you we would be good together. I lied. We're dynamite."

Seven

Sunlight streamed through the windows, falling across Victoria's eyes. She stirred, stretching as she awakened. Her lashes lifted, her gaze unfocused. Her bedroom was different. The feel of a weight across her breasts made her glance down. Cord! She was fully awake now, remembering. Smiling, she turned her head to find Cord watching her. There was a shadow of a beard on his chin, his dark hair was ruffled from sleep and his eyes were half-closed but alert. He looked delicious, all male and pleased with all he surveyed. If she hadn't suspected she was wearing a similar expression, she might have teased him about it.

"You smiled. You're happy?" Half question, half statement.

"More than I can tell you." She lifted her hand to his face, brushing her fingers over the stubble. The rasp of bristles on her skin was surprisingly erotic. "How long have you been awake?"

"Too long. And not long enough. Do you know that you tuck a hand under your cheek when you sleep?" He had watched her sleep, feeling more contented than he had ever been in his life. In fact, until this moment, he hadn't really known what the word meant.

She grinned. "No, I didn't. Is it important?"

He wanted to tell her what he was feeling, yet he couldn't. He settled for a half-truth. "Maybe not to you but it is to me." He cupped her breast, teasing the nipple that pouted in its center. "I wanted to make love with you, but you looked so peaceful I couldn't wake you. It took forever for the sun to do the job for me. And the more I watched you, the more I wanted to see."

Victoria's amusement slipped away. Tenderness eased in its place to soften her body, to touch her emotions in new ways. She slipped her arms around his shoulders and drew him to her. "I enjoyed last night," she whispered. "I've never felt so special or found so much pleasure in loving."

"I'm glad." He brushed his lips across her breast, tasting her once more. The desire that he had slaked again and again through the night was still with him, but it was gentler now. Time had ceased to matter. She was here and there was no rush. "I wanted it to be the best it has ever been before."

Victoria inhaled softly as he suckled. The pulling motion created sensations of pleasure and an ache deep within her body. Yet his words held her attention. She frowned a little as the meaning sank in.

"You speak as if I have known many men." The thought disturbed her for a reason she hardly understood.

"It doesn't matter. I'm no virgin. I don't expect you to have been before you were married."

Instead of feeling reassured, Victoria was even more disturbed. She took his head in her hands, lifting it so that he had to look at her. "I have only known one man before you and that was George," she said, searching his expression. "Why would you think that there were more? Why would it matter?"

Cord tried to pull away. She held him close. He had meant to reassure her not disturb her, making her ask questions. "Are you trying to change the subject? I had other things on my mind," he asked, hoping to deflect her.

"Answer me, Cord." Victoria knew his tactics too well to be taken in.

"You were twenty-two when you started working for me. Virgins are fairly rare at that age. Then there was George. You met and married him in less than six months. You must have been sleeping with him." He shrugged, trying to ignore the anger stirring to life when he thought of the others who might have held her in their arms, might have drunk from the well of passion with her in the dark of the night.

Victoria just stared, feeling the tension invading his body. His eyes were alive with emotions. "I don't understand you," she said, groping for a toehold on what was happening between them. "Do you always handle your affairs like this?"

Cord did pull away then. "This isn't an affair," he grated, getting out of bed and going to the window. He glared at the landscape, seeing more than he wanted to of his past liaisons. "There is no similarity between you and the women I've known. We have more than I ever had with them. I like and respect you. We're partners." He swung around, hating the need to explain.

Victoria sat up in bed, tucking the sheet around her. The nakedness of her body hadn't bothered her until now. "You didn't like them? You took women to your bed you didn't respect?" She looked at him, frowning at the images he invoked. She understood other men using women but not Cord. She didn't want to think him so insensitive.

"No! Damn it! I did like them." He raked his fingers through his hair, frustrated, angry. "I don't know why I started this. It wasn't the same with them. I'm trying to tell you that I don't think of you as one of a list of bodies. That mattered to you last night."

She remembered then the words she had thrown at him. Now she understood. He was trying to reassure her. She forgot her nudity. Throwing back the covers, she got up and went to him. She slid her arms around his waist and pressed her body against his. "Cord, I don't mind having an affair with you. I know we have more than most people who sleep together have. Why do you think I had such a time deciding to come to you?" She lifted her head to smile at him. "Can't we forget everything that is supposed to happen in this kind of arrangement, the things each of us is supposed to say, and just enjoy what we have? It is special. I know it. You said it."

He looked down at her. His hands came up to smooth the tousled hair back from her face. The light

shone over her, highlighting her dark eyes, gilding the
ivory skin with gold. Why did he hesitate, he wondered. Her warmth was wrapping around him as
surely as her scent clung to his skin. He wanted her
more than he had ever wanted a woman, any woman
in his life. Yet an affair didn't seem enough. In a way,
it almost seemed a betrayal and that he didn't understand.

"You can't be content with that? First a virgin then
a wife. And now this."

She laughed softly. "You don't need to make it
sound as though I'm some sort of extinct species. Stop
worrying." She shook him a little, trying to tease him
out of his mood. "I remember you telling me that I
could start a whole new life if I wanted to. I could just
wipe George and all my past out of my mind and start
over. That week you brought me out here, remember? I can finally do it. I want to do it. Starting today,
starting now."

Cord resisted her for a moment longer, then he bent
his head and took the lips she offered him. There were
still questions to be answered but not now. He was a
fool. He didn't know what was driving him to seek
answers for questions that popped out of nowhere to
plague him. But no more. He had Victoria now. For
as long as they wanted, for as long as their passion
held them together.

"So what shall we do today?" Cord asked. He
stroked Victoria's hip, enjoying the feel of her skin. He
was more relaxed than he could ever remember. He
didn't really want to move from the bed. Yet as fan-
tastic as their lovemaking had been, he wanted to just

be with her, laugh with her, talk, or sit quietly somewhere.

Victoria raised her head from his shoulder. "I don't know. You pick. We could stay here. I'm sure we could think of things to do."

He smiled at her, seeing the lingering passion in her eyes. That she was so free with him was a delight. "Wanton."

"I know. Isn't it terrible? I never knew I could be so demanding." She lowered her lashes, aiming for a demure expression and failing completely. There was something inherently impossible about being shy and innocent when one was lying in one's birthday suit so close to one's lover. A breath could not have slipped between her and Cord. She liked the closeness that he seemed to want after the lovemaking was done.

"I never knew friendship was such an advantage in an affair," she added in a throaty whisper.

Cord rolled over, trapping her beneath him. "So you want to play games, do you?" He nipped her ear just hard enough to send shivers of delight racing over her skin. "I've just decided what I want to do. You could pack us a picnic lunch, and I'll take you fishing."

"Fishing?" Victoria's eyes popped open in astonishment. "You're kidding, I hope. I don't know how, and frankly, I can't see you sitting still long enough to fish or to teach me."

"I'll have you know I'm a fairly good fisherman, not that I get too much practice." He grinned at her. "Are you game, or don't you think you can take it, city woman?"

Her chin came up. "I can do anything I set my mind to," she informed him, knowing he was challenging her just to corner her into agreeing. "And don't think I don't feel you setting me up," she added, when he chuckled and gave her a hug that had nothing to do with passion. "It would serve you right if I fixed you a peanut-butter-and-jelly sandwich."

"You won't. For one thing I don't have any of that stuff in the house." He dropped a kiss on each breast before rolling out of bed and pulling her with him.

Victoria wrapped her arms around him, nestling her body in the cradle of his hips. "Are you sure you won't change your mind?" she teased him.

He shook his head, enjoying her sultry act. "Nope, but you're welcome to keep working on me." He bent and lifted her into his arms. "In the meantime, let's take a shower together and conserve water."

Victoria tucked her head against his throat and gave herself into his keeping. She found it strangely satisfying to be carried by Cord. She liked the way he touched her even when they weren't making love. His affection was new. He had always been scrupulous about how he handled her until now. She liked the newfound freedom this affair was giving them. She smiled a little, remembering her reservations. She had been a fool. She should have known Cord would never hurt her and that being with him would only add to her life.

"I am not going to stick that thing on that hook. It's still alive." Victoria stared at the poor worm and shuddered.

"It's bait, Victoria. I told you, you can't fish without food." Cord efficiently dealt with the hook and tossed it over the side of the boat. The bobber immediately popped to the surface, ready to give the signal the minute there was a bite.

"You also can't catch fish without the proper equipment. And these stick things aren't it."

Victoria brandished the pole she held like a weapon. She watched Cord try to contain his laughter while she stifled her own grin. Since they had gotten into the boat and floated a short distance down-water from the house, she had been teasing Cord. The picnic lunch was packed, minus the peanut-butter-and-jelly sandwiches. She was suitably garbed for the outing in an old shirt of Cord's and a pair of jeans she had left from the last time she had stayed at his home.

The morning was clear, the mist from the bayou faint wisps that lent an otherworldly quality to the setting. If she looked over her shoulder, she could see the house Cord had designed. It blended beautifully with the wild landscape without being diminished by the beauty surrounding it.

"What are you thinking?" Cord asked quietly, gazing at her. The half smile on her face was almost secretive. He couldn't remember ever being so fascinated by her expressions.

Victoria looked at him, her expression reverting to the devilish mood that had been on her since she had seen the kind of fishing expedition he had in mind.

"I was wondering whether there are any alligators in this water."

They both knew she was lying.

Cord glanced around, then pointed to the opposite bank. A long granddaddy-of-them-all lay sunning itself. "At least one," he said, allowing her to change the subject. Maybe it was better if he didn't delve into her mind too much. Knowing Victoria, she would hit him with a reciprocal question. And he just wasn't prepared to guard his answers. He wanted this time with her without the complications they had already faced.

He picked up his pole again and motioned for her to do the same. "Do you think we could get started on catching our dinner?"

"All right." She grimaced before gingerly baiting her hook. "What do you say to a little bet as to who catches the biggest fish?" Cord always liked a challenge.

Cord gave her a sharp look. He hadn't missed how well she had managed just then. "I'm not getting hustled, am I?" he demanded suspiciously.

"Who me?" she replied with such studied innocence even she didn't believe it.

"Victoria Wynne, if you live to next year it will only be because you ran faster than I did," he muttered, glaring at the bobber that sat on the surface of the water without moving.

"Not up to the challenge?" she teased, following suit.

"Unlike you I can refuse a dare," he returned, without looking at her.

"We'll see."

And see they did. Victoria caught one fish. Cord caught one. If they had been betting, neither would have won. The size and the number were evenly divided between them by the time they decided to call it a day. The sun was high in the sky when Cord beached the boat on shore. Willows drooped to shade the bank he had chosen. Wildflowers grew more profusely than in a garden, scenting the air with a fragrance unrivaled by any perfume. The day was silent as though waiting. Even the bayou lay sleeping, resting in the midday spring warmth.

"It's beautiful here," Victoria murmured, not wishing to disturb the peace. "I don't know how you can bear to come back to the city. The traffic alone is enough to drive a person wild."

Cord spread the quilt on the ground. "It's too quiet sometimes," he admitted as he straightened. "I come out here every weekend to recharge, but I'm usually glad to go back on Sunday night. I guess I'm just not cut out for a peaceful setting." He shrugged before joining her on the blanket. "I like the challenge of urban life and the sometimes hectic pace."

"Didn't you ever bring anyone out here with you?" If she hadn't been watching him, she would have missed his hesitation.

"No."

Victoria thought that over. "Ever?"

His eyes held hers as he shook his head. "You're the only one I ever brought here. I built this place as a retreat. I sometimes need to get away from the business, the noise, the demands on my time. I resent them occasionally. Some people are free. Some have to work at it."

"And you're one of the ones who have to work at it. Why?" she invited softly. There would never be a good time to ask what she must. Now was the best she could hope for. "What drives you? What makes you so careful around people, so distanced with most of your relationships?"

He stiffened, glancing at her. "That's a fairly harsh statement. When have I been distanced from you?"

"I'm not talking about myself in that number and you know it. Talk to me, Cord. I need to know more about the man who makes such exquisite love to me. Is that so strange?" The words hurt because she knew he didn't trust her enough to give without reservations.

"I wish you would let it be. Isn't today enough? Nothing else matters."

"I think it does." The lovely mood was broken. She regretted the loss, but she needed to understand.

Cord got to his feet and walked to the water's edge. He stood gazing down at the river. She had a right to ask, he admitted to himself. But did he want to open the locked door of his memories? He knew what waited there. She didn't. He turned. She watched him and said nothing more. He knew she had pushed as far as she would. Their relationship was built on a strong foundation. Could he trust it enough to tell her? Trust. A small word. Sometimes an impossible dream. Sighing, he walked back to her.

"Is this a condition to us?" He had to know. He saw the pain in her eyes and had his answer before she spoke.

"No."

He dropped onto his knees beside her, taking her hands in his. "That wasn't fair."

"No, it wasn't," she agreed huskily. "But you needed to know."

The silent implied why was more demanding than a shout would have been. "It's a long story."

"I'm not going anywhere." She held onto him, needing his strength without knowing why.

"It's funny, but now that I've decided to tell you, I don't know where to begin." He paused. "My parents divorced when I was twelve. I was a big kid, strong, tough and smart. All the teachers in school said so. So did mom, and dad while he was with us. When he left my mother, my younger brother, Robert, and me, there wasn't a man in the house anymore. No one to fix the plumbing, handle the lifting, help with Robert, mow the grass. That sort of thing. Mom cried a lot. Robert was three years younger than me and constantly in and out of trouble at school."

Victoria could guess what was coming, but she didn't interrupt. Cord needed to tell his story his way.

"Somehow, I became the father. The older I got the more Mom depended on me. Robert was her baby. Anything he wanted, we tried to give him. I loved him, but for some crazy reason he was jealous of anything I did. Not that I did all that much. There wasn't time. Mom and I both worked two jobs to help support us.

"Anyway, Robert would swing from being repentant and grateful to me for standing by and digging him out of his messes to blaming me for his need to prove himself. Mom was constantly caught in the middle. I wanted to be an architect. There was no money so the only way I could do it was a scholarship. Even that became a bone of contention between Robert and me. He didn't want to go to college, but he resented the fact that I had won a grant so I could. His resentment turned to rage. He broke into a small ap-

pliance store and got caught. I was twenty at the time.
I can still see my mother's face when the police came
to tell her Robert was in jail. The trial was a horror.
All kinds of things came out. He had been bilking our
neighbors out of money for years, especially my
friends. My mother was humiliated. We tried to pay
back what he had taken. Half our so-called friends
were pathetically *grateful*." He bit the word out, his
face contorted.

"The other half didn't want anything to do with us.
Robert went to jail for the first time." He paused,
drawing a deep breath. He looked at her, almost prepared to see pity or revulsion in her eyes. All he saw
was compassion and understanding.

"And you felt guilty." The need to cry for the boy
he had been was strong. Admiration for the man he
had made of himself grew deeper. Cord could have
become embittered by his background, or cruel.

"Wouldn't you?" he demanded harshly. "I was so
tied up with my life that I didn't see what he was
doing. My friends, the people who had helped us when
we needed it, had been taken in by my own brother. If
it had stopped there, it wouldn't have been so bad. But
it didn't. He quickly got out of jail. First offense and
all of that. He promised Mom he would go straight.
She believed him. I did too, fool that I was. Nine
months later there was another cop on the doorstep.
Another crime, only this time a confidence scheme
that had gone bad. Robert went back to prison, and
Mom couldn't take it anymore. She just gave up after
that. A year later she was dead. A year after that,
Robert was on the streets again. He came to me. More
promises. This time I had sense enough not to trust

him. He went to a friend of mine who had just started a small business. Scammed him out of what little cash he had and skipped town. It took me a year to pay him back."

She had always wondered why a caring man like Cord would willfully turn himself into a loner. Now she knew. "So you choose your friends carefully, people you think can't be easily cheated or taken in, men like James Southerland."

"Not consciously perhaps, but that probably doesn't make it any less so. Robert is still out there somewhere. Every few years he turns up like a bad penny. I don't want any more people I care about hurt by him."

Cord had expected to feel the pain in the telling. He hadn't expected to feel relieved. He looked at her, seeing the sheen of tears in her eyes. He wanted to take her in his arms and hold her. She was the most beautiful thing in his life.

"Where's Robert now?"

"I don't know. I moved away from Chicago, that's my hometown, the minute I paid the last debt. I saw Robert just before I left and told him I wouldn't be around to pick up the pieces anymore. He didn't believe me."

"So you came here and built Darcourte Architect, Inc.? Not bad for a self-made man," she said softly, sliding across to him. She needed a deeper contact than just holding his hand. She thought he did too. "Why were you so determined not to tell me? Did you think it would matter to me that you have a criminal for a brother?"

"I don't know. Maybe. It mattered to a lot of people whom I thought would have judged me for myself."

"I don't care. I care that you had such a hard time growing up, that you had to watch your mother's disillusionment and live through your own. But I don't care about who you're kin to. I never will."

Cord wanted to believe her. The past had taught him too well. "Robert is like a sword hanging over my head. He could make trouble for me in a number of ways. That's one of the reasons I've never wanted anyone in the firm with me. Until you. Logic went out the window the first day I saw you. It hasn't come back in since." He glanced at the river rather than at her. She meant so much to him. "Robert never lost his jealousy of me. If he sees that I have someone like you, someone who means a lot to me, he'll move heaven and earth to hurt you just to injure me. I couldn't take that. He is my brother. For all he's done, he still shares my blood."

For just one moment, she had allowed herself to hope. Cord had finally given her his trust. She had thought the telling meant the barriers he had erected between them were toppling. Now she saw the problem was much deeper than that. He was protecting her, whether she needed or wanted it.

"We could handle him together if the need ever arises. I'll grant you his reputation could cast a shadow on ours, but not enough to worry about. You're too established here. We both know that." Pride meant little to her now. She believed in Cord and herself. He had taught her that.

He shook his head. Her soft voice, the scent of her on the breeze, the touch of her hand in his. Temptations. He could have her. All he had to do was reach out and take what she offered, what he wanted.

"Why not? Put it into words, Cord," she challenged him.

He turned, angered at her prodding. "Trust me to know him better than you."

"So we have an affair and that will keep me safe from him?" She rose to face him, angry now.

"I don't know. I shouldn't have brought you here. I should have left you alone and let you find someone who wouldn't hurt you." He started to move away.

She caught his arm, dragging him around to face her. "I don't need you to guard me from the big bad world. I'm a grown woman, not a child. I make my own decisions. Sure George bent me up a little. But I was young when I married him. I had stars in my eyes and stupid, impossible dreams in my heart. I don't believe in fairy tales anymore. I look at you and I see more than you give me credit for." The tears flowed down her cheeks, but she didn't feel them. Her very being was focused on Cord. He had to hear her.

"You don't know what you're saying. You don't know what the gossip is like, the words people you trust whisper behind your back. The way they stop looking you in the eye. The way business associates start scrutinizing your work to make sure the blood tie isn't coming out in your estimates."

She shook him hard. "You're seeing things in the worst possible light. But that's not the main issue anyway. I won't let you throw the business up as a smoke screen, nor will I allow you to pack me away on a shelf to be protected at all costs." She released him, almost throwing his arm away from her. Stalking to the picnic basket, she plopped down on the quilt. Right now there was no way to show him how wrong she thought he was. "Let's eat. I'm starved. Arguing with a mule always gives me an appetite."

Cord stared at her, unprepared for the change. "You're not serious."

"I am." She dug into the basket and pulled out two plates. If Robert had been sitting beside her right then, she would have taken great pleasure in telling him what kind of a man she thought he was for what he had done to Cord and to his own mother. If there was any justice in the world, the man would get his reward.

"You expect me to eat now?" he demanded, taking two steps toward her.

"You're going to need your strength if you intend to hold me off, Cordell Jackson Darcourte." She looked up at him with fire in her eyes. "I've just declared war on male stupidity. To be specific, yours." She waved a celery stalk at him like a weapon. "I'm sticking with you. You dragged me back from George. Now it's my turn. What are friends for?" The smile on her lips wasn't nice. It promised more trouble than he had ever had.

Cord studied it, speaking slowly. "Why?"

"I'll let you know when I find out."

"Supper was delicious. I'd forgotten how well you can cook," Victoria commented, leaning into the cushions Cord had thrown on the floor in front of the fireplace in the den.

They had finished supper and chosen to relax in the study, Cord's favorite room. A fire burned in the hearth to ward off the faint chill of the evening. The house was quiet as the day drew to a close. Victoria sat curled against the pillows she had tossed before the hearth. Cord stood at the window looking out.

"What's wrong? You've been quiet all day." She studied his rigid back, trying to understand his silence. Cord was never silent. If something bothered him he confronted it. She had never fought for anything but her career in her life until now. Cord was so important to her. She wanted him as she wanted no man. She loved him. Simple. To the point. No frills. She loved him, had, in fact, for months. When had it happened, where and how? She didn't know. Oddly, it didn't seem to matter now.

What did matter was that he didn't seem to love her. Oh, he cared, more than many men who married women they desired, she suspected. But Cord wouldn't let himself love anyone. She didn't need him to tell her that, to know the truth. Saddened but not discouraged, she knew she would do everything in her power to change his mind. He had taught her strength and courage. He had made her believe in the future when he didn't believe in it himself. He had forged the steel that would ultimately slay the dragon of his cynicism. She didn't know how she'd win, but she would win or know she had done everything in her power to touch the man she loved, a man who lay buried beneath the past.

Cord turned, looking at her. The firelight gilded her skin with a ruby glow. Her eyes were fixed on his face, her hands still and graceful in her lap. He wanted her so much. She made him feel whole when he wasn't sure he even liked himself very much. She made his shadows seem like illusions and that worried him. They were very real.

"Are you regretting us?"

"That should be my question." He came to her, sitting down beside her so that they were at eye level.

She smiled, relief coursing through her. He wasn't angry. He wasn't brooding, either. Two steps in the right direction. "I'm not regretting anything with you. I never have, although you do try my patience to the limit." She touched his face, outlining his jawline and then his lips.

"You're playing with fire. Why?"

"Why do you think?" She looked at him through half-closed lashes. The heat of desire was weighting her limbs. Slipping her arms around his neck, she nestled deeper into the pillows.

"I don't know. I wish I did. You're different." He frowned even as his hands cupped her breasts. Her scent teased his senses, her skin was living silk in his hands.

"You don't like?" she whispered, her voice a deep purr of enticement.

He bent his head to her lips. The fire had painted them ripe as cherries waiting to be picked from the tree. He wanted her taste on his tongue. He wanted to lose himself in her softness, to feel her pulse around him as he carried her over the edge of passionate madness. He wanted...

He kissed her, blotting out the rest of his thoughts. His world was shaking on its axis. Her hands held him, softly, gently, yet demanding that which he had given to no one. He didn't want the demand, but he couldn't resist the temptation of her body. He told himself he could control her fire and her temper. As he joined them as one, he wondered if he were lying to himself. Every time he touched her he found he needed her more. *Need. Trust.* The words haunted him. He had given her one. He couldn't give her the other. He would need no one.

His breath was coming fast as he drove over the edge. Her cry was sweet on his lips as he found his own release. He lay with his head pillowed on her breast, feeling the chains of need slipping around him. He wanted to fight her and their passion. He raised his head, his body tense.

Victoria felt the change even before she saw the storm in his eyes. Because she loved him she took a chance. "We are dynamite in the sack, my friend," she murmured, daring to tease him, knowing he hoped for words that were more serious, words he could fight. She watched him blink, then shake his head as though to clear it. His eyes narrowed suspiciously. She smiled at him, hoping he wouldn't notice that she was almost holding her breath. Her smile widened naturally at his subtle relaxation. She had averted the crisis that she had only sensed.

"That we are, friend," he agreed. He caressed her breasts, his fingers lingering over the soft curves as though to stake a claim.

Victoria heard the emphasis he placed on the word *friend*. It hurt to know he had needed to make the distinction. But oddly, it gave her hope too. Why should it matter to him if she weren't becoming more important than he wanted to admit?

Eight

"Which apartment? Yours or mine?" Cord stood beside the door, looking relaxed but feeling anything but. "Or would you rather stay here and drive back in the morning? I don't mind. Remember, it was your suggestion that we leave tonight."

Victoria slipped on her light jacket, smiling a little at his tone. "You may like getting up at the crack of dawn, but I don't. The idea of driving into town to get home to shower and change early enough for me to take my nine o'clock appointment is not something I want to face. I like leisurely mornings. Not hectic ones."

He opened the door for her, then locked it behind them. "Did you enjoy yourself this weekend?" He glanced at her as they walked to their cars.

"You know I did." She paused beside hers.

He watched her in the moonlight. "So where shall we go? Or would you rather be alone?"

"No, I would rather be with you," she admitted after a small hesitation. She slipped into the driver's seat, blessing the darkness of the interior that hid most of her expression. She hadn't expected it to be so difficult to answer a simple question.

"Good choice but where?" He laughed softly when she didn't have an immediate answer. "Still shy with me after this weekend?" He leaned over to tuck a tousled lock of hair behind her ear after he shut the door.

The gentle caress rippled over her skin, reminding her of the passion they had shared less than an hour earlier. "Maybe a little," she confessed finally. She laughed at her awkwardness. "My inexperience is showing."

"Not in any place it matters," he assured her, bending to kiss her affectionately. "I want to sleep with you in my arms. Believe it or not, I've never said that to another woman. If you hadn't agreed, I would have had a hard time getting the words out to change your mind." He gave her the truth, wondering how much longer he could keep their relationship on a friendly level.

His breath whispered over her cheeks, bringing warmth to ward off the cool of the night air. "That helps."

"My place or yours? Your choice. Although, come to think of it, my bed is bigger than yours," he teased in a husky whisper.

"I can't help it if I'm not six-four," she returned smartly, while angling her head in a silent invitation for a more demonstrative reason for sharing the night with him.

Cord read her well. "You have too many moods, darlin'." This time his kiss sizzled. He was breathing hard when he lifted his head. Her soft moan of protest made his body tighten in response. "You took too long. I choose my place. We can pick up some clothes for you on the way."

"What have you done to Cord?" Maybelle demanded, stealing into Victoria's office. She shut the door after peeking first up and down the hall like a spy on the trail of state secrets.

Victoria looked up from the Jansen plans she was working on. Thursday mornings always seemed to be the busiest of the week. "What are you muttering about?" she asked with a frown. "What has Cord done?" She cocked her head to listen but heard nothing but silence.

Maybelle threw herself into a chair, rolling her eyes heavenward. "That's just it. Cord hasn't done anything."

Victoria laughed. "Don't make it sound so impossible. He never was that bad and you know it. He's just a bit temperamental."

Maybelle gaped. "Only you would describe him as a bit temperamental. Do you have any idea how unnerving it is to wait for him to stop looking so pleased with himself and the world? I just know he's up to something. I've worked for him for twelve years, and I have never known him to go for four days without an explosion of some kind. Even when that subcontractor ordered pine instead of cypress for the Southerland terrace, Cord barely said a word."

"Don't pin any medals on him. I distinctly remember you muttering about having to call all over the parish looking for someone who could fill the order."

"But it's not the same thing," Maybelle argued, her plump hands waving about as though they would explain more clearly what she could not.

"Are you telling me you would prefer him stalking the corridors like a wounded moose?"

"It sounds stupid, doesn't it? His temper never made me nervous. But his grin and the compliments he's been tossing out definitely do."

Victoria felt like laughing again but smiled instead. "Don't worry. Something is sure to set him off soon," she promised. Privately, she was thrilled at the change in Cord. It wasn't just his mood that had mellowed, but he seemed less restless, more content with himself. The brilliance was still there, the drive, the ambition, but it was more in control, less demanding.

Maybelle stared at her, suddenly struck by a thought. "You two aren't..." She stopped, floundering for words.

Victoria let Maybelle stew for a moment. She wasn't trying to hide their relationship. She was proud that she and Cord were a pair, that he cared for her. If it were up to her, she would have shouted their relationship from the rooftops. But she couldn't crowd Cord. She knew very well he was sure that they were simply engaged in a friendly affair.

"We are," she said finally. Maybelle's discretion was one of the reasons she had lasted so long with Cord.

Maybelle's mouth formed a perfect O. "No wonder he's been so different. Now I can stop waiting for
the bomb to drop."

The slang tricked a chuckle out of Victoria. Her
brows rose. "Cord does have some distinct similarities to an explosive," she admitted.

"Victoria!"

Both women glanced to the closed door. Cord
knocked once then entered before Victoria could answer. "Those fool cleaners have done it again. Come
look at my desk. I can't find a thing. I thought you
had them fired." He leveled a look at Maybelle. "You
did get us another firm, didn't you?"

Maybelle nodded before getting to her feet. "I did.
They've been on the job for almost ten days now
without a problem."

"Well, there's one now," he muttered. "I can see
myself in the reflection on the desk. If I had wanted a
spray-wax commercial, I would have hired a movie
company not a cleaning firm."

Victoria stood up, wondering how she worked in a
madhouse. Walking over, she tucked her arm in
Cord's. "Come on. I'll help you find your plans if
you'll get that new nursery owner I mentioned to you
to give me a decent discount for the Jansen project. I
swear the man is kin to a French pirate. He's trying to
rip me off and I don't like it. And what's more, the
jerk is one of those old-liners that think a woman
hasn't got a brain in her head." Indignation showed in
her expression. She knew her comment would raise
Cord's ire, giving him something else to focus on besides the disruption of his office. She and Maybelle
were running out of reputable janitorial services.

"Then don't do business with him. There are other nurseries in this city we can use."

She shook her head. "No way. He's got the best selection of plants I've seen. Quite a number of exotics." She stopped on the threshold of Cord's office, half expecting to see papers strewn all over the floor. There were a few littering the desk, but that was all. "I can't believe it. This place doesn't look as if hurricane Cord struck."

He chuckled. "I thought I would give up swearing and working up a head of steam. I beat the cigarettes, so I figure I can change a few old habits, too."

Victoria studied him, thinking he looked a bit too pleased with himself. "What are you up to?" she demanded, becoming as suspicious as Maybelle at his abrupt change in behavior. "Are you sick or something?"

"What a question. Can't a man improve himself without the woman in his life coming apart at the seams? If I had known you were this attached to my disposition, I would have worked on getting surlier," he grumbled.

He had wanted her to be pleased with his restraint, especially about the smoking. When he thought of all the times he would have walked a mile for a cigarette and had made do with gum, he wanted to swear. He stalked to the storage cabinet and started searching for the plans the cleaners had moved. On second thought, maybe her usual perception had a reason to be lagging. He had kept her very busy of late. His temper died as the memories of how they had spent their time surfaced. What were a few missed cues against the excitement of passion?

Victoria followed him, caught between laughing at her own and Maybelle's inconsistency and Cord's indignation. "Don't do that," she said, grabbing two tubes of plans before Cord could toss them over his shoulder. "I'll look for the drawings. And I'll even apologize for not appreciating the effort you're making."

Cord turned his head, giving her a grin. "I got you."

Victoria blinked at the change. The gleam in his eyes demanded a retaliation, but she was fresh out of ideas. "Cordell Jack—"

The rest of his name was lost in his kiss. When she came up for air, she was in his arms, her hands buried in his hair. "That's unfair tactics," she murmured in a husky purr.

"That's the understatement of the year."

The intrusion of another voice had Cord and Victoria glancing toward the hall. James came into the room, shutting the door behind him. "I see you two have finally managed to get together." He sat down and crossed his legs at the ankle. "Don't mind me. I don't have anything to do this morning."

Victoria pushed at Cord's arms, but he only held her tighter. Since she was half bent over, her lower body pressed intimately against his, there was little leverage to be found.

"Cord!" she snapped, trying to keep dignity intact in an impossible situation.

Cord ignored her to focus on his audience. "Do you mind? We're busy. Go away and bother someone else. We don't have an appointment with you today."

James laughed, enjoying himself. Victoria looked ready to explode, and Cord looked remarkably like a warrior protecting a battle prize. "I can see you're busy. Don't let me stop you. I'll just wait until you finish. Maybe I can pick up a few pointers." He couldn't resist teasing them.

"I don't give lessons," Cord drawled with awful patience. He turned his head to look at Victoria. Her glare was eloquent. He sighed. "I'm getting a lock for that door tomorrow. Remind me to use it." Lifting her upright, he released her.

Victoria smoothed her clothes, aiming her annoyance at both men. "You two remind me of boys showing off on a playground. I ought to wring your necks."

James tilted his head. "I think the lady is angry at us."

"I don't get angry, I get even," Victoria inserted before Cord could comment. "You better watch your backyard. Remember James, I am landscaping your house. Be careful, or you might find a yard full of cactus and passion plants."

Cord slipped an arm around her waist, enjoying her fire. James looked as if a favorite pet had just reached up and swiped at his nose. Cord dipped his head to kiss her, staking his claim and sharing his delight with the woman responsible. "And what do I get for punishment?" he demanded.

Victoria knew his weakness. "Fast-food takeout for a week."

He groaned. "That's ten times worse than James's penance. You know I don't like assembly-line food."

Victoria slipped out of his hold and perched on the edge of Cord's desk. "You want to try for two weeks?"

"Not on your life." He moved to his chair and made a stab at being serious. He couldn't remember a time in his life when he had enjoyed just waking up in the morning. Victoria had brought a freshness to his existence. By nature, they were both intense, committed people. Yet, since they had become lovers, a change had overtaken them. They played more now, laughing at little things, finding fun in situations that ordinary people bypassed.

"So what brings you down to see us?" Victoria asked when Cord made no move to discover James's business.

"I'm giving a party a week from tomorrow. I wanted you to come. And I wanted to check on the house. I haven't had time to get out to the site in the last few days."

"It's coming along fine. The contractor has finished the exterior work. The windows are in. The drywall-and-paneling people started yesterday."

"How long before they're done?"

Cord hesitated then asked, "I thought you told me a couple of weeks ago that there was no longer any hurry about finishing. There was even some talk about selling the place. Has something changed?"

"I'm in no rush, but I've changed my mind about getting rid of the place. Just because Suzanne and I aren't together anymore doesn't mean I don't want the house. The farther I got into the actual designing, the more I realized I'm tired of living out of an apartment. I want a little room and some privacy."

Victoria met Cord's eyes, seeing her thoughts reflected there. James's voice held more determination than sincerity. She rose and started for the door. "I need to get back to my work. All this extracurricular activity is putting a crimp in my schedule."

"I don't mind if you stay."

She shook her head as she passed James's chair. "No. You talk to Cord. I'll see you next week." She glanced at Cord. "We are going, aren't we?"

"We are as long as there's dancing."

"You hate dancing," two voices said together.

"Well, I've changed my mind." His look left no one in any doubt as to why.

Victoria felt the heat of his gaze down to her toes. She had to get out of there or James would see more than just a little fooling around.

Without a word, she sought refuge in her own office, shutting the door behind her. She took a deep breath and released it. How much longer could she go on before she gave herself away? Every time they made love she fell more deeply in love. Every time Cord smiled at her she worked that much harder at making it possible for him to relax. The man who could play and tease was emerging slowly. She couldn't pinpoint the exact moment when she had begun uncovering the depths she glimpsed in Cord. She only knew her need existed and was growing stronger every day.

"Cord, if you don't tell me where we're going I'll expire of terminal curiosity." His laugh wrapped around Victoria in the close confines of the car. "You had me get dressed up for something."

"I told you it's a surprise. Besides, I like the look of that rose-colored silky thing on you. I even like those earrings, although I wish you would let me buy you real jewels instead of those elegant fakes." He grimaced at the term. Victoria was adamant about holding on to her independence. Their largest fight to date had been over her insistence on continuing to pay the bills on her apartment when she was hardly there. He should have been glad she was trying to keep at least part of their lives separate. No affair went on forever. Yet he didn't want to think about this one ending. He didn't want to think of a time when there would be another woman in Victoria's place.

Victoria flicked the teardrop earrings with a forefinger. "I'll have you know elegant fakes are the rage."

"Well, you should be in diamonds. Maybe I'll get you some for Christmas. Everyone gives presents on Christmas," he added in case she was marshaling her objections.

Victoria sat up straighter. "You will not. I know you. You'll go out and buy the best diamonds you can find. They'll cost a fortune."

"Are you impugning my taste?" he tried to joke. Damn it, he wanted her to have the best. What was wrong with that? She was his woman. He had a fortune, one that he had made himself. He could spend it any way he wanted. However, he knew better than to tell her all this.

"You have perfect taste and you know it. What I'm saying is that I don't want you buying me things. I'm not going to haul out the cliché about being a kept woman. I think more of both of us than that. But I am going to demand the right to give as equally as I get. I can't match you financially and we both know it.''

"I don't care about that.'' He frowned. In all the words that had flown back and forth between them, she hadn't given him this reason.

"But I do.''

Cord didn't answer for a moment. He understood, even though he could not agree. Saying goodbye to the mental image of her in his bed naked but for the diamond earrings was difficult. "All right. No earrings. It's too early to be thinking about Christmas, anyway.'' He'd find a way around this little snag without hurting her pride.

He pulled into the small parking lot near the riverbank. A few yards away a diesel-powered replica of a stern-wheeler lay at anchor. Lights decorated the structure. Dixieland music spilled out of the open doorways and windows while the costumed crew mingled with and greeted the guests coming up the gangplank.

"I do like your surprises,'' Victoria stated, taking in the scene. "I've always wanted to ride on one of these stern-wheelers. I can't believe I've lived here all this time and never done it.''

"We'll have dinner and do a little dancing,'' he promised her, helping her from the car. "We'll be cruising the bayou for five hours to the tune of Dixieland. I hear the food is great, so I hope you brought your appetite.'' He grinned at her excited expression.

"You've got dancing on the brain.''

"That and a few other places. I like holding you in my arms. This way I get to do it in public as well as in private.''

Victoria leaned her head against his shoulder. The breeze stirring small waves on the Mississippi was cool, but she hardly noticed. "I like the way you think. Bring on the music. I love my surprise."

Cord leaned down, taking the lips begging to be kissed. Victoria had sensuality and femininity down to an art form.

Victoria tasted Cord like fine wine. It didn't matter that strangers watched from the shadows. It didn't matter that they weren't alone. All she knew was the feel of Cord's body against hers, the gliding touch of his hand against her back and the stroke of his tongue along hers. Lovemaking was all the more enjoyable for its restraints. The desire built in her slowly, glowing without burning, lying in wait for the fuel it really needed, privacy and time.

"We'd better get on board," Cord whispered against her lips as he raised his head.

"I know," she whispered back. "I love..." She stopped, swallowed, then tried again. "I love my surprise," she said, repeating herself.

He flicked her chin with his forefinger. He missed the slip in the pleasure of having his gift accepted. "I'm glad. I wanted to give you something special."

She wanted to tell him he already had but buried the words. For one moment her lashes dipped to hide the sheen of tears in her eyes. Then she made herself smile. She had more than she expected, and as long as there was a tomorrow, there was hope for more.

"So tell me all about this boat. I want the Cook's tour," she commanded, determined to enjoy the moment as he had taught her to do.

"I bought you a book." He pulled a small bro-
chure from his pocket and handed it to her as he urged
her up the ramp. "I knew you'd want to know every
little fact. You always do."

Victoria squeezed his arm. Cord hated research. "I
was beginning to think you had changed beyond all
recognition. I'm glad I was wrong. I—I..." she
stumbled over the word. "Like you the way you are."

Cord glanced at her, slowing their progress up the
gangplank. "Do you really mean that?"

"Of course I do." It was almost impossible to understand how Cord could believe she hadn't cared for
him as he was, that he felt obliged to alter his personality for her.

"I have the devil's own temper."

"So what? So do I. You can handle it. So can I."
She tugged on his arm. "What I don't like is missing
a meal." If she didn't change the subject, she was
going to cry. Could he be coming to think more of her
than friend and lover? Every wish she had ever had
was tied up in the questions in her mind.

As the evening progressed, she found herself
watching him, searching for a hint of the depth of his
feelings for her. She found desire, passion, enjoyment, respect and liking. She saw no sign of the love
that filled her, almost killing her with its intensity.
How could he not know, she wondered, as they glided
together across the dance floor? How could he not feel
the special rapport they shared and not recognize its
source? How could he be so blind? She wanted to
shout "Look at me! See me as more than your friend,
your lover."

The surprise that Cord had planned had begun with such promise. Now it was a bittersweet experience. When Cord suggested they leave, she was glad to agree.

"You're very quiet. Tired?" Cord took Victoria's hand and carried it to his lips without taking his eyes from the road ahead.

"A little," she admitted softly. "It has been a long week." Better to make conversation than to think in silence.

"One more day, then we can go out to the bayou. Do you want to leave for the country after work tomorrow or get an early start on Saturday?"

Victoria frowned. She hadn't thought that far ahead. The idea of two full days in Cord's company without the diversion of their hectic schedules should have been heaven. Instead, it was a challenge she wasn't certain she had the strength to meet. His every word, every look, every gesture conjured up so many possibilities. How much longer could she keep her love hidden? It was becoming more difficult every day.

"I really need to catch up on some chores at my place—"

"Okay. We'll stay in town this weekend and I'll help you."

She stared, taken aback at the offer. In her experience a man did not offer to help with the laundry and vacuuming. Suddenly she wondered what it would be like to have Cord in her life on a permanent basis. After George, she had all but promised herself she would not marry again. "I don't want to ruin your time off."

"What about your time off?" He frowned. "You know it might not be a bad idea to think about getting a cleaning lady."

"Can't afford it. At least not yet."

Cord glanced at her carefully. Would she go for it? The only way to find out was to ask. "There is one way you could cut down on your outside work. I have a maid."

Victoria wished she weren't so familiar with how Cord's mind worked. "I don't think Mrs. Lovell would like being shared by us. Two apartments are twice the work," she murmured.

"That's not what I meant." He paused, searching for words. After what George had done to her, Victoria had every reason not to want to share her life with a man for a long time, if ever. Despite their closeness, they both knew there would be problems in living together. Neither of them had found compromise easy, but for the sake of their relationship, they had made it work.

Victoria held her breath, hoping. Was he easing around to making a commitment? If Cord had changed, then so had she for even considering accepting such a tie.

"It doesn't have to be anything formal. You could still keep your place if you wanted. It would be easier on you if all your things were at my apartment."

Disappointment was a bitter pill. Cord still needed an out. It was bad enough to know he kept a large part of himself from her, and now this. Breathing slowly, carefully, she searched for an answer.

"I don't think that's any different than what we have now." She jerked slightly as Cord swung the car off the road and cut the motor.

He turned to face her. "Are you satisfied with what we have? We're neither really living together, nor are we apart. It's like being in limbo."

She couldn't commit herself until she was sure of him. She had come a long way but not that far. "Are you?"

Impasse.

Cord groped for the words to explain his feelings. Only for Victoria would he try. "I've never wanted someone to come home to. I want you. Is that enough?"

Anguish, mingled with need and hope, was in his eyes. Cord was a strong man with enough courage to ask for what he could have taken. But there was still that wall of aloneness, that place he kept protected even from her.

Victoria framed his face with her hands. It wasn't a legal union he was proposing. It probably wasn't an admission anyone but she would recognize. "I don't care how or where we live. Really I don't, but I don't think this would be right for either of us. You like your solitude. One day..." Her voice trailed away as words failed her.

Cord sat still. He hadn't expected her refusal. The disappointment was more pain than it should have been. It took a moment for him to fight the need to demand she agree. She had the right to choose.

"If that's the way you want it." He touched her face, wanting to take her in his arms and convince her otherwise.

"It is." She hurt. Perhaps she should take what he offered. Perhaps she should try to build on that, but she couldn't. Without his love, she wouldn't be able to live with him day after day, and she knew she would never be able to hide her own love from him.

Nine

Come on honey, rise and shine."

Cord leaned over Victoria, waiting for that moment when she would open her eyes and smile at him. Her body was curved into his, snuggled against his side. She was warm, soft and yielding. It was hard not to make love to her until they were both late for work, but he restrained himself. They had gotten in late the night before and had spent too many enjoyable hours pleasuring each other until it was almost dawn.

He smiled slightly as she murmured in her sleep and cuddled closer. His arms tightened and she relaxed. He couldn't pinpoint the moment when he realized that to have her sleeping beside him was more than just comfortable, warm and arousing. She felt *right* pressed against him.

Sometimes he wondered if she wasn't too right in his arms and in his home. He was beginning to need her; maybe he had always needed her but wouldn't admit it. He had asked her to live with him, telling himself that he only wanted a deeper affair. She had refused and continued to refuse his request. In many ways he respected that, but he also didn't like the fact she could make a separation that he no longer was capable of. He needed...

His thoughts slowed, groping for a toehold on exactly what it was he did need. Cord looked down at Victoria's face, seeing vulnerability, a woman's strength and gentleness. When she awoke there would be fire to match his. But here, now, she was tame. His body tightened, the desire that never seemed to diminish growing stronger as the sun crept across the sky. Understanding himself no longer seemed to matter.

He bent his head to blow gently against her ear. If she didn't get up soon, all his good intentions would go out the window. "Unless you want to be ravaged again, wake up," he whispered.

Victoria smiled sleepily, wriggling her bare bottom against his hips. "Cord, you're either going to kill us or turn us into sex fiends," she mumbled, trying to push her mind into high gear. "You know it takes me forever to function. Don't make propositions I can't handle until after I get my eyes open."

He kissed her. He couldn't resist when she wore that pouty expression. "Do you want to be late?"

Victoria managed to focus on his face. "I don't care if I go in at all," she admitted, winding her arms around his neck. "Want to play hooky with me?"

Cord had taught her how to play. She enjoyed waking up in his arms, seeing the desire darken his eyes, feeling his hands on her body, giving and taking pleasure. She had never known lovemaking until Cord. George might have initiated her into the sex act, but Cord had taught her the beauty of making love.

Cord lightly teased one nipple until it hardened. "Don't tempt me, witch. I have a living to earn and a reputation to keep up." The wicked gleam in her eyes made him laugh. "Don't you dare say it."

Victoria tried to look innocent. "Say what?"

Cord got up, pulling her with him despite her protests. "You know what, thorn in my side." He urged her toward the bathroom. "If we hurry, we can take a bath together."

"The last time you had this idea we ended up at the office at eleven, and I have a ten o'clock appointment today." She accepted the turban he handed her and stuffed her hair inside. If they hadn't really needed to get to the office, she would have taken a shot at changing his mind.

Cord turned on the taps to fill the tub. "We'll be quick this morning. I promise."

"Where have I heard that before?" Memories of other laughingly broken promises filled her mind. Her nipples hardened, liquid heat stirred responses she tried to control. Just looking at him gave her ideas.

Cord kissed her again, lingering over her lips as he stroked her satiny skin. Her shivers whispered of her rising need. He smiled, feeling his body respond. "But this time I have a reason to keep my word. Maybelle is threatening to quit if you remember."

Victoria tucked her head under his chin as she snuggled closer. "I remember. I also remember the reason had nothing to do with us being late. It had to do with your sloppy habits. Wasn't it something about it being the absolute last time she would go to bat for you with the cleaning company?"

Cord frowned at her. "Am I really that bad in the neatness department? Maybe I ought to work on that next." He stepped into the tub.

Victoria slipped in beside him, inhaling softly at the water-slick feel of his body moving against hers. The sensation was highly erotic, bringing with it images of the last bath they had shared. Loving him was the most exquisite torture on mornings like this. How easy it would be to blurt out her feelings, how useless. For one moment pain rippled beneath the pleasure before she could protect herself against it.

She made herself remember what she did have with Cord. "No, you aren't really that bad, and don't you dare do any more changing. I'm having a hard enough time keeping up with you as it is. I told you I like who you are, so stop worrying." She poked a finger at his chest. If she kept up with the nonsensical conversation, she might be able to forget the desire heating her blood, the love twisting for freedom in her heart.

"Besides if you keep aiming at being perfect, I'm going to have to change a few habits of my own. And I like having a neatness fetish. And it won't be half as much fun if you suddenly turn up being Mr. Clean. Who would I grumble at? And if I changed that habit, the next thing I'd want to work on would be my slow way of getting out of bed in the morning."

"No, you don't." Cord gathered her closer still, ignoring her finger. "I like the way you wake up. It would ruin my day not to see your smile when you're dreaming and then that pout when you realize dawn has come again. I'd even miss you grumbling at me when I tickle you awake."

Victoria laughed, rolling so that she was half lying on him. "It's a good thing this tub's so big."

He chuckled huskily. "That depends on the activity you have in mind. Right now it's not big enough." He stroked her bottom when she bumped her hips against his. "Behave woman and start washing. The clock is creeping up on us." He handed her a washcloth.

"Spoilsport."

"Desperate man. Give me one kiss to hold me."

"No way. We *will* be late then and you know it."

"I don't care. I've just changed my mind about work." He tossed their washcloths out of the tub and hauled her against his chest. "I should have known better than to think I could be in here with you without having you."

"Yes, you should have known better," she agreed, molding her body to his. She was delighted to know he was no more able to cage the passion between them than she was.

She took his lips, needing him, wanting him, loving him. Every time he touched her, she learned more about herself and him. Every time they came together, her love deepened until she no longer knew where it began or ended. She arched against him as his lips found her breast. She inhaled sharply.

"Now, Cord," she whispered, surging against him. "Make me yours now."

Desire sizzled in a moment. The water swirled while the minute hand marched on. Two became one in a rush that sent a wave crashing against the porcelain tub to splash onto the floor. Neither noticed. The world had narrowed to just the two of them.

They were late to work again, but that didn't matter either.

"I swear it's a good thing our customers are used to you both getting tied up on one site or another," Maybelle muttered on seeing them enter the office. She glared at them impartially. "I want you to know that if I have to bend the truth for either of you one more time so you can waltz in here looking like two cats that have been at the cream bowl, I want hazard pay. One of these days someone is going to realize that I'm lying and call me on it."

Cord grinned. "You've been threatening for years to leave me to deal with my clients when I blow your appointment schedule. You know you don't mean a word you're saying."

Maybelle made a rude noise. Victoria chuckled, trying to hide the sound in a cough. "We're sorry," she apologized, ignoring Cord's wicked expression. She wasn't sorry at all and he knew it.

"In a pig's eye you are." Maybelle flipped her calendar page around so they could see the marks of rescheduling. "See that? You're going to be lucky to get out of here by five. And Cord, you told me you wanted an early afternoon. I'm not a magician." She folded her arms.

Victoria glanced at Cord. "I told you," she murmured, unable to resist the temptation to tease him. The twinkle in Maybelle's eyes was reassuring. They were in no danger of a secretarial revolt.

"Ladies shouldn't kiss and tell," Cord returned, giving her a look that could have boiled water.

Maybelle enjoyed the byplay. "I'm getting to be a regular con woman with our clients. If they only knew the fibs I tell in a good cause," she said with a laugh.

Cord's grin died. He turned to examine the secretary carefully. Maybelle's comment had hit too close to home for comfort, although she couldn't know about Robert, for he had told no one in New Orleans but Victoria.

Victoria knew immediately what was wrong. Cord was upset over such an innocent comment. She caught his arm. "Listen, before you get started, I want you to have a look at the last set of Jansen's plans." She started down the hall. It didn't matter that she was leaving Maybelle behind wondering what she had said. All she was interested in was the look on Cord's face and the memories the secretary's words had triggered. She shut the door behind them as Cord shrugged off her hold.

"You don't need to baby-sit me. I'm fine."

Victoria went to him and put her arms around his waist. He was tense against her, but he didn't push her away.

"Stupid, isn't it? Just for a minute there, I wondered if she knew." He shook his head.

Victoria watched his face. She had to know. "Did you think I might have told her?"

He stared down at her. "No."

Victoria released the breath she had hardly been aware of holding in a rush. "Thank you for that."

His arms came around her. "I trust you." This time his tone was deep with sincerity and emotion.

Victoria laid her head against his chest, knowing she was one step closer to her goal. The knowledge was pain and pleasure. So close and yet so far.

Cord held her, absorbing the fact that it hadn't even occurred to him to wonder if Victoria had confided in Maybelle. Why hadn't it? He let her go without looking at her. "Do you have anything for me to look at or was that just an excuse?"

Victoria felt the change without understanding the cause. She knew better than to ask for explanations now. He would tell her when he was ready, if at all.

"No."

"Then I'll see you later."

He was gone before she could object. Victoria stared at the door for a moment, then went to her desk. She had work to do that couldn't wait. The first hour was the most difficult. She kept waiting for Cord to stop in or buzz for her. Finally, she realized he wouldn't. Whatever was bothering him, he was fighting it out on his own. Burying herself in the plans she was working on, she tried to blot out her disappointment.

A knock at the door interrupted her. "Come in," she called without glancing up.

"Are you planning to skip lunch today?" Maybelle asked from the doorway.

Victoria glanced at her watch and then at the secretary. "I didn't realize it was that late. Where's Cord?"

"I think he went out to the Southerland site."

"Oh." She and Cord had a tentative lunch date if their schedules had permitted. Was Cord avoiding her? The thought found fertile ground in her mind, resisting her efforts to push it away.

"Are you going to lunch?" Maybelle repeated her question.

"No, I want to finish these. You go ahead. I'll keep an eye on the office."

Maybelle hesitated, wanting to say something but deciding against it. "If you're sure."

Victoria nodded. "Go. But could you bring me back a sandwich if you have time?"

Relieved, Maybelle smiled slightly. "Chicken salad?"

"And a pickle."

After Maybelle left, Victoria sat staring out the window. She had lied. The plans for the Jansen landscaping were complete. She could have eaten with Maybelle, but she hadn't wanted to discuss Cord's behavior.

"Is anyone here?"

Victoria started at the male voice coming from the outer office. "Coming," she called, rising.

She entered the waiting area to find a man examining the room. He was shorter than Cord by at least an inch, but it was his face that held her attention. Cord's features, a little rougher cut perhaps, and Cord's eyes, slightly faded. The style of his clothes was expensive as was the Rolex on his wrist.

"You must be Victoria Wynne." The man stepped forward, his hand outstretched.

He even moved like Cord, although not as gracefully, she noted vaguely.

"I'm Robert, Cord's brother."

Victoria accepted his hand, hiding her amazement at his appearance and the casual way he walked back into Cord's life. She wanted to toss him out on his ear but hid her reaction with a conventional remark. She wasn't sure why she was making the effort. Instinct? Woman's intuition?

"You look very like him."

He laughed softly. "A compliment from a lovely lady. My lucky day."

Victoria's smile felt strained as she detached her fingers from his grip. Without thinking about it, she knew she didn't like the man and wouldn't have trusted him without or with her prior knowledge of his dishonorable past. "Cord's not here right now."

Robert's face fell, his disappointment blatant. "I should have called. Cord is always so busy." He stepped back as though he intended to leave.

"Have you come far?" Victoria asked. Her mind was racing. Why was Robert here? What did he want? How much did he know about Cord?

"Farther than was comfortable. Travel these days is an exercise in frustration. Hurry up and wait." He sighed and picked up the bag sitting at his feet.

Victoria caught the slyly probing look he leveled at her as he bent down. Hiding her increasing dislike, she asked, "Where are you going?"

He looked surprised. "Why, to check in to a motel. Then I'll call back in later to see if Cord has returned. I don't want to be a nuisance, which I would be if I hung around here until my brother returns."

Victoria recognized the role-playing. The gestures, the reluctant expressions, the disappointment, all very well done, too well done. Robert's questionable charm next to Cord's honesty was no contest. She couldn't imagine how anyone could prefer or believe Robert over Cord.

"Perhaps you'd like to leave your number," she suggested, missing what she suspected was her cue to offer to let him stay.

The mask slipped for a moment. "Maybe I'd better wait after all."

Victoria made a pretense of looking around. "If you wish. The chairs are quite comfortable, but I don't know how long Cord will be."

"I could wait in his office."

Victoria shook her head. "He wouldn't like that."

"Or yours. I'd hate to interfere with your clients."

Disturbed by his tone, Victoria frowned. Was that a threat? It sounded like one. This was the very situation that Cord had feared. She couldn't leave Robert in the lobby saying heaven only knew what to whomever walked in. "Perhaps you're right. How about using mine?"

He gave her a charming smile. "I much prefer the company of a beautiful woman to the anonymity of four walls and a bed."

Victoria gestured toward the hall, feeling unclean from the effusive compliment. "It's this way."

"This is a very impressive setup. Cord always did have good taste."

Ignoring the probing remark, Victoria sat down at her desk. She decided to play dumb. Perhaps the man's ego was big enough to like playing up to the little woman. She didn't like the tactic, but she was prepared to use it for Cord.

"You mean you haven't been here before?" She wondered if he would admit the truth.

Robert's expression was rueful. "I'm afraid Cord and I have been at odds for years. More my fault than his." He spread his hands, looking awkward. "I'm the black sheep of the family. You obviously know Cord well, and you can imagine what his opinion of me is. And he's right. I have done some things Cord disapproved of."

"Why are you telling me this?" She watched him closely.

Robert hesitated. "I have a confession to make."

Now they were getting to the crux of the matter. Robert was getting smoother by the second. She didn't know much about con artists, but she had a feeling he was moving in for the kill.

"I want to reestablish myself with Cord. We're both older now and I'm wiser. I want to mend my fences. But I know Cord well enough to know it won't be easy." Robert held up his hand, silencing Victoria before she could speak. "I didn't mean to make it sound as if Cord would be so unforgiving. It's just that I've given him no reason to be."

"I don't think you should be telling me. It's Cord you should talk to," Victoria began, making the expected protest.

"Believe me, I know." He tried a smile that didn't quite succeed. "You see, I checked into Cord's background before I risked approaching him. I didn't want to mess things up for him. You two are very close according to the people I spoke to. You must have some feel for his personality. I was hoping I could call on you to help me get Cord to see reason." He leaned forward as he confided, his eyes showing both admiration as well as vulnerability. "It's time Cord and I acted as brothers, not enemies. Since it's my fault we're estranged, it's my pride that has to go on the block."

If Cord didn't get back soon, she was going to be sick to her stomach. No wonder Cord hated lies. "Cord's my friend and my partner. My first loyalty is to him," she said evasively.

Robert's hopeful expression faltered then died. "You won't help me?"

"I don't see how I can." Victoria shook her head, working at showing regret for refusing.

Robert glanced down, heaved a sigh, then looked at her. "It was worth a try," he replied, looking dejected.

"I have some work to finish. Do you mind?" She had done her best. The rest was up to Cord. Whatever Robert wanted, she wasn't the one he would tell.

Robert shook his head, looking disappointed. "Not at all. I'll look at these magazines. You go on and pretend I'm not here."

"Victoria, I'm back."

Victoria froze at the sound of Cord's voice. She had time for a quick glance at Robert's face. The malicious satisfaction written there made her wish she had left him to rot in the outer office. She could hear Cord's footsteps in the hall. If it had been possible to spare him this, she would have. She rose and came around the desk.

"Have you had lunch yet?" Without waiting for a reply, Cord entered the room to take her in his arms.

His kiss was deep, long and hard. For one moment she remained stiff in his arms. Then the hunger he made no effort to hide got to her, heating her blood and driving out all other considerations. Her hands threaded through his hair. She took what he gave and returned it full measure. When she came up for air, she had forgotten they had an audience.

"No, I haven't had lunch. Not that you deserve to have me wait for you. You left and I wasn't sure when you would get back."

He grinned at her indignant expression. Her eyes held equal measures of irritation and desire. He liked knowing he could blow her poise when no one else could. He hadn't missed the slight resistance she had put up. "There was a problem on the site."

"And you didn't think of anything else but that. Not very complimentary, my friend."

He chuckled and kissed her again. "I'll make it up to you, I promise."

Victoria pushed at his arms, not really angry but prepared to tease him a little before she admitted it. Her eyes settled on Robert as Cord released her. Passion faded. She glanced at Cord just as he turned and saw his brother. The change that settled over his face was dramatic. His lighthearted mood died. His features set in hard lines, his eyes darkened.

"What are you doing here, Robert?" The question was harsh, demanding, with suspicion underlying every syllable.

Robert rose, his smile apologetic and pleading. "I came to see you. To make peace."

"Peace!" Cord drew away from Victoria to study his brother. The past had taught him just how far he could trust Robert. But he couldn't forget, even now, that the man was his only remaining relative. For that, he would listen one more time.

"What kind of peace?"

Robert glanced at Victoria as though to apologize. Victoria hardly noticed. Her attention was on Cord. She didn't want him hurt.

"I had hoped we could be friends, make a new start." Robert put on a pleading expression.

Cord watched him, seeing more than he wanted to see. "Are you in trouble?" he asked, the possibility being the only reason he could think of for Robert's change of heart. "I meant what I said the last time, I won't clean up your messes anymore."

Robert's eyes narrowed, anger turning his face a deep shade of red. "I'm sorry, Victoria. I didn't mean to spoil anything for you," Robert said through clenched teeth. "I guess I should have known this would never work."

Victoria knew Robert was trying to force her to plead his case. She moved closer to Cord, determined that there would be no doubt in either man's mind where her sympathies lay.

Cord looked down at her, wanting to touch her but forcing himself not to.

"I think you should be on your way," he suggested, glancing back at Robert.

Reading the menace in his voice and expression, Robert leaned down to pick up his suitcase. "I'm going, Cord. But I'll be back. You can count on it."

Cord watched him walk away, knowing that for his sake and for Victoria's he had to find a way to stop living with the threat of Robert's return always hanging over his head. Victoria was right. It was time to get his freedom. Just for a moment he let the sadness and regret of what his brother had become hold sway.

"You would think after all this time I would stop wishing he would change. He makes me so angry, and yet I can't forget that we were born of the same mother and played together as children."

Victoria tried to imagine how she would feel in Cord's place. She wasn't certain she would have listened to Robert. "I'm glad you care even after all he's done. I think that's one of the things that makes you so special to me."

He shut his eyes for a moment, then opened them to pin her with a look. He reached out to stroke her cheek with his fingertips. "Am I really special to you?" He needed her as he needed no one else, yet even now he couldn't tell her so.

Victoria held back the words of love aching for expression. She would not trap him with her emotions. "Very special." She put her arms around him, holding him, needing to be held by him.

Cord allowed himself to find peace in her arms for one moment before reality intruded. Robert was out there somewhere, sizing up his next victim. But this time things would be different. Robert's last prison term shouldn't have been up for two more years. That had to mean something.

"I want you to go home. Wait for me." He pulled Victoria away from him to look into her eyes. "I have to find out what he's up to. I can't leave things like this."

"Let me help you."

He shook his head. "No. Robert's my problem not yours. I must do this alone."

Victoria felt the pain of his rejection down to her toes. It came down to trust. Cord was still protecting her, still holding himself aloof when he could have reached out.

"If that's the way you want it," she murmured, going to her desk to pull out the plans she'd just finished. She couldn't look at him, for if she did she would plead for a place at his side. "If you don't need anything else, perhaps I can get back to work." She stared at the drawings through a haze of tears. She knew he was watching her. She waited, wishing he would leave, hoping he wouldn't, hoping he would by word or gesture reach out to her just once. She needed him to share with her, not push her away. She had been so sure he was coming to need and trust her. Now she wondered if she hadn't been fooling herself because she wanted his love so much.

The door clicked shut. She lifted her head. She was alone. And so was he. By his choice.

Ten

___

Victoria entered her apartment and kicked off her shoes, tossing her jacket on the chair near the door. For the first time in days she was alone, really alone. The apartment felt as empty as she did. There was no warmth here. No love. Cord had asked her to wait for him, but she wondered what she was waiting for. She had handled so much with him, but she couldn't take his need to push her away. On one level she understood it. He was trying to protect her from Robert. But she suspected he was also protecting himself from needing her. She hadn't expected that. She had thought he would be glad she had seen through Robert.

Sighing wearily, she undressed and got into the shower. The night stretched before her. She wasn't sleepy, so there was no escape from her thoughts. Her concentration was shot, making work out of the question. And brooding didn't appeal. She wandered into the kitchen, trying to decide what to have for dinner. The doorbell rang as she stood in front of the refrigerator. Her eyes lit with hope. Cord had come. Slamming the refrigerator door, she hurried to the entrance.

Excitement and the beginning of a smile died. "Robert!" The last person in the world she wanted to see.

"May I come in?" he asked hesitantly, glancing past her as though looking for someone.

"Why?" Her fingers tightened on the knob as she blocked his way.

"I came to apologize to you. I had no idea I would be interfering in your life when I asked you to help me mend my fences." He watched her speculatively.

Victoria frowned. The more she saw of this man the less she liked him. "I don't know what you mean."

"I know you don't. Could I come in so I can tell you why I did what I did?" He edged closer, crowding her subtly into the small foyer.

Victoria hesitated. There were a number of reasons why she shouldn't listen to him, but she ignored them all. Robert was the key to Cord. She'd use anything to find a way to help him.

"All right." She stepped back.

Robert passed her to enter the living room. He stood there awkwardly as though he didn't know what to do next. Victoria's sympathy should have been stirred at his show of unease. All she could remember was Cord's face when he had told her the stories that showed this man's complete lack of conscience.

"You'd better sit down," she said quietly, taking a seat across from him. Maybe if she got him talking this time, she would find out exactly why he had come. Forewarned was forearmed.

Obeying, Robert looked at his hands for a few moments before he raised his eyes to her. "May I tell you about myself? Will you listen now? It will make the rest so much easier to explain."

Victoria pretended to consider. "I'll listen."

Robert sighed deeply, relaxing in his chair. "Thank you. I don't deserve your forbearance after the trouble I caused."

"What makes you think you caused me any trouble?" She kept her voice neutral only by willpower.

"I know Cord. We are brothers. I know he hates the thought of me. He has the devil's own temper. And since you are the closest one to him . . ." He stopped, grimacing at the slip. "I'm sorry. I shouldn't have said that. But it's so obvious you love him. I didn't mean to pry, really."

"I don't wish to discuss my relationship with you. You said you had things to tell me. Please do so." She barely stifled her irritation. She gave Robert credit for one thing, he had seen the love Cord was blind to.

"Now I've made you angry." Her look was a warning. "I am what you might call a confidence man. I've been in prison. I'm out now, but while I was there I learned a lot about myself. I'm trying to go straight. I wanted to see Cord and try to patch things up between us. You would never know it as things are now, but when we were young we were very close. As I started taking the wrong turns, Cord had to pick up the pieces of the things I did. I was younger by three years and I wanted so much. Our family was middle class, not wealthy. I discovered early how willing people can be to help those they liked. I don't know when I crossed the line from honesty to shaving the truth, and one day it became even more than that. My behavior caused a lot of gossip in the small town where we lived. The trial wasn't easy on Cord or my mother. She's dead now. I can't make things I did up to her, but I can try to make my peace with Cord. That's why I'm here, the only reason I pushed myself into his life. He has every right to be ashamed of me. I know that. But I had to try." He paused to look at her pleadingly. "You can understand that, can't you?"

Victoria stared at him, amazed at how plausible Robert made the past sound.

"So what do you intend doing now?"

"I'll try again. I thought if I could meet Cord on some neutral ground, I might have a better chance. The only thing is I don't know New Orleans or his habits very well."

Victoria ignored the opening. What was driving the man? Money was the obvious answer. How much and who for? Two questions, and no way to get answers without admitting how much Cord had told her. "How long are you staying in town?"

Robert frowned. "For as long as it takes, I guess."

It wasn't difficult to figure out what Robert was thinking. His disappointment was cleverly concealed, but she felt it. She wished Cord were here. It was time to face Robert down. It was time someone took Cord's side and didn't leave him to pick up the pieces of Robert's careless path through life. She wanted to be that someone. Not because Cord had given her so much, had been there for her when she needed him, but because she loved him. She wanted his freedom from the sword of Robert above his head. Whether he loved her or not, he deserved his freedom.

Cord drove toward Victoria's apartment, remembering her face when he had told her to go home and wait for him. He knew she wanted to share the burden of Robert with him. He knew, also, that in many ways he wasn't being fair in not allowing her a place at his side. The rationale that she had enough trouble in her own life wasn't good enough. The truth was he needed to be alone. He needed to face his feelings for his brother. The trip to his lawyer's hadn't been easy. Telling the man what and who his brother was had been the least of it. Knowing that he was considering turning his brother in for breaking his parole, knowing that by doing so he was condemning Robert to a prison term with little hope of release or parole in the near future, were bitter pills. But he was through being used. He was through allowing Robert to tear into his life and the lives of others. The law was very explicit. Robert was a habitual criminal. His parole was contingent on his good behavior.

After leaving the lawyer Cord had made a few phone calls and pinned down the probable reason for Robert's appearance. Now all he had to do was find his brother. That had been the stumbling block. No amount of phoning had produced where Robert was staying. Frustrated, angry, and missing Victoria, Cord had given up for the day. Cord parked his car across the street from Victoria's apartment building and got out. He paused, staring up at the lights shining in the windows. He had a lot of explaining to do. Was she missing him? Would she understand his need to face Robert alone? She had given him so much, and now he was asking for more.

Cord started walking, then paused in midstride as a man came out of Victoria's apartment. Cord inhaled sharply. Robert! With Victoria! Late! Her home! How did Robert know where Victoria lived? What was he doing there so late? The questions raced through his mind as he closed the distance.

Eyes slitted in a mixture of worry and temper, he glared across the space. Victoria stood silhouetted in the doorway. They spoke, but he couldn't hear the words. Then Robert smiled. Cord knew that smile. It meant he'd won, that someone else had been taken in by his act. His Victoria would be hurt. Clear thought, logical action was impossible. All he knew was that Victoria was alone with Robert, unprotected. This was one person who would not be hurt by his brother.

Victoria glanced up to see Cord stalking toward them. The light of the streetlight illuminated his expression. Pure rage. She stepped toward him, hoping to reach him before he reached Robert. She barely made it. Catching his arm, she halted his advance.

"Cord. I've been waiting for you," she whispered. She wanted to touch him, but his closed expression put her off.

"Have you?" He stared down at her. "What has he been saying to you? Did you invite him here?"

She shook her head, accepting the thrust of his temper even as she felt the pain. "Of course not. I wouldn't do that to you."

Cord searched her expression, seeing the truth written in her anxious eyes. He relaxed slightly, wishing he hadn't asked the question. He should have remembered Victoria could have betrayed his confidence with Maybelle and hadn't.

"What are you doing here?" Easier to look at Robert than at Victoria.

"I thought I would see you sooner or later," Robert said, stepping closer to Victoria's door. "Maybe we should go back inside. There is a nice fire in the fireplace. And I know how you don't like to have our little visits in a public place."

Cord knew his tricks, knew Robert's words were calculated to needle his temper. He fought the barbs. This was one game he meant to win. Catching Victoria's arm, he urged her indoors. "Cut the pleasantries. You know why I'm here."

Robert shut the door and leaned against it, watching him. He ignored Victoria. "Showdown time. And with an audience. Want to prove your manhood?"

Victoria said nothing. She could feel the tension in Cord's hand. His fingers were tight on her arm. She had wanted to put her hand in his, to stand beside him as he faced down his past. She had gotten her wish but not in the way she would have wanted it. Cord hardly knew she was there. And Robert was using her to hurt the man she loved.

"Maybe I should leave you two alone," she began quietly.

"A good idea," Cord agreed.

"No. Stay. If you're going to keep sleeping with him, you might as well know the rest of the family.

Besides, I might settle here, and you wouldn't want to pretend we haven't met." He smiled at her.

Cord watched him, listened to his oily words. "You aren't moving here. And Victoria won't ever see you again. Nor will I."

"Oh, are you planning on disowning me again? You tried that once. It didn't work then and it won't work now." He sauntered to the couch and sat down.

Victoria rubbed her arm as Cord released her to take a step toward his brother. His hands were clenched at his side. He looked ready to take a good swing at Robert. Victoria knew the feeling. She couldn't believe the hatred in Robert's expression or his voice. How Cord was holding on to his temper was beyond her.

"I won't have to disown you. I made a few phone calls after you left the office. Found out a lot of interesting facts. Things like the big gambling debt you owe to some not-so-forgiving people in Vegas. The wealthy widow you met there, who just happens to live just outside of New Orleans on a very large estate. But the most important bit of information that I turned up was that this time you're out on parole. Have you forgotten the rules already? I realize it's your first time as a model prisoner released for good behavior."

"Cut the sarcasm. That's my forte, not yours," Robert snapped irritably. "So you found me out. Big deal. You know you won't do anything about it."

"Think again. I've already put the wheels in motion. I would even have given the police your address if I had it."

Robert stared at Cord, stunned at the turn of events. His face turned an ugly shade of red as his temper exploded. "I'll get you for this."

"I doubt it. You're going to be much too busy staying out of the way of your creditors. Men in prison can't pay back large sums of money." Cord didn't like what he was doing, but Robert had given him no other choice.

If Robert had been red before, he was now pasty white, his eyes glazed with shock. Victoria watched, hardly able to believe the scene. She had never seen Cord this cold and in such perfect control. Without raising his voice, he dominated the room, making Robert appear the caricature of a man. If she hadn't known Cord so well, she might have thought he was glad he could turn his brother in. Instead, all she could see was the pain in his eyes as he did what had to be done. Her love bloomed deeper and richer for the strength he displayed.

Robert swore, long and hard. Cord stood there, his arms folded across his chest taking it all. "You've said your piece. Now get out."

"I'll get you for this," Robert blustered, getting to his feet and hurrying to the door.

Cord watched him go, hating what he had done and wishing things could have been different.

"I'm sorry, Victoria," he stated quietly without looking at her. "I had hoped to keep you out of this."

Victoria wrapped her arms around her middle to ward off the chill of his words. "When are you going to learn that I want to share everything with you? The good and the bad. Do you have any idea how I feel right now? You shut me out. I would have been at your side, but you shut me out.'' The tears stood in her eyes, demanding release, but she fought them back. ''I have shared my life with you, not just the pleasant things but the ugly, too. Some of my best memories have been tied up in those times, and yet you deny me the same gift.''

Cord looked at her then, seeing more pain than he wanted to know. ''Don't you think I know that? You have suffered enough through George. I won't let you suffer through me.''

''You're a fool, Cordell Darcourte. I love you, you great ox. But I won't be put in a glass case and protected like a useless doll by you or any man. I won't sleep with you, share with you, only in health and happiness. I need more. I need you in all ways and I'm not afraid to say it. But you are.''

Cord reached out to her. She slapped his hands away before he could touch her. ''I didn't mean to hurt you.''

''I know that.'' The tears spilled over to run down her cheeks in silent streams of grief. ''That makes it even worse.''

Cord spread his hands. ''I can't take back what I did.''

''And you wouldn't even if you could.'' She said the words she knew he would not.

He wanted to lie but had never given her less than honesty. Finally, slowly, he nodded.

Victoria slumped against the wall, suddenly tired beyond measure. ''Then there is nothing more for either of us to say. Please go.''

''Just like that? This is the end for us?''

"It has to be. I want more than you can give. I thought I could be content, but I found you have taught me too well." She smiled bitterly. "The ultimate irony. You taught me to go after what I wanted and not to accept second best. You taught me not to look to anyone else for my needs, to find strength in myself."

"I love you, you know." He spoke quietly, almost dispassionately.

"I know." She shook her head. "This time it doesn't make any difference. Just go." She closed her eyes so that she wouldn't see him leave. Where she got the strength to send him away, she didn't know.

The click of the door closing was loud in the apartment. Victoria held her position for a long moment, not even sure she was strong enough to undress and climb into bed. Tomorrow would come whether she was ready for it or not. She would have to face Cord day after day or run. And she would not run. He had taught her that, too.

Suddenly she saw her future stretched out emptily before her. The picture was too much. Burying her head in her pillow, she cried until there were no more tears. Sleep was a reluctant companion and the morning too soon in coming. She dressed for work without caring what she wore. Makeup hid some of the damage of the night, but nothing helped the ache in her heart.

Could she face Cord today? She stared at the clock. Every cowardly impulse demanded she call in sick. She couldn't forget the way he had turned from her in one of the most painful moments of his life.

His car was in its usual slot. Victoria sat staring at it. Could she walk into the office and pretend he had never held her in his arms? She had to try. It took more nerve than she thought she had just to get from the parking lot to the reception area. The sight of Maybelle's frown when she saw her did nothing to help her mood.

"What's going on around here? Cord is in a temper you wouldn't believe," she said, glancing behind her and down the hall. "Did you two have a fight or something?"

"Or something," Victoria admitted, heading for her office, hoping to escape before Maybelle got the curiosity bit between her teeth.

Maybelle followed her. "Well, whatever it is, go make up. I've never seen Cord look so—" she spread her hands in a helpless gesture "—I don't know. It's in his eyes. They look empty."

Victoria forced herself not to react. She was barely pasted together as it was. All last night and this morning, she had lived with the hope Cord would call her. "I can't. We don't want the same things. It's over." Bending, she pushed her handbag into the bottom drawer of her desk. Anything to keep her hands busy and to look as if her heart weren't breaking.

Maybelle sat down with a thump. "I don't believe it. That man is tail over teakettle in love with you."

Victoria reached for the stats for the new job she was taking on. "Sometimes love isn't enough. Trust is important. And sharing." She took off her jacket and got ready to work.

Victoria could feel Maybelle's eyes on her, but she didn't look up. She didn't want to see her pity or sympathy.

"Are you all right?" Maybelle asked softly.

"I will be eventually." This time she lifted her head to give Maybelle a strained smile. "Contrary to popular belief, I won't die from what ails me."

"I still don't believe this." Maybelle frowned. "Are you sure you didn't misunderstand?"

"I'm sure." Leaning her elbows on the desk, she propped her chin in her hands. "He wants to wrap me up and keep me safe from the real world. I can't live like that." The bitterness and the pain were in her words.

Maybelle's brows rose. "I know he's a bit overprotective where you're concerned, but that's just Cord. It's natural for a man in love to protect his woman."

"And who protects him? Who holds him when he has a problem? I can't be just a fair-weather lover. I need to give as well as take."

"Maybe you're not giving him the benefit of the doubt. Cord is more open with you than anyone. Give him a chance. Or isn't your love strong enough for that?" Maybelle demanded grimly.

Startled at the harsh tone, Victoria stared at Maybelle. "I gave him many chances."

Maybelle stood and planted her hands on her hips. "So give him more. You two belong together. You're a fool if you can't see that. Trust has to start somewhere. Why don't you start by believing that one of these days he'll share all the things you consider so important? There are worse fates in the world than having a man so besotted with you that he would take on the world to keep you safe.''

Something in Maybelle's voice caught Victoria's attention. ''You know about Robert, and what Cord did?''

Maybelle nodded. ''His lawyer called this morning to say that the police were closing in on Robert. I took the message because Cord hadn't come in yet. I don't know the details, but I do know Cord, and I can imagine what it took for him to turn his brother in to the police—whatever the reason. And then there was you.''

Suddenly, Victoria was seeing herself in a new light and not liking the image. Had she asked too much of Cord? Maybelle's words held a truth she couldn't deny. Cord did give her more than he gave to anyone else.

''Where is he now?''

''Holed up in his office.'' Maybelle stalked to the door. ''Nursing his wounds. I don't know what else. He won't let me near him.'' She walked out, slamming the door behind her.

Victoria stared into space, wondering what to do. She had hurt Cord and herself last night. She wanted desperately to put things right, but even now she wasn't sure she could. How much could she accept from Cord without giving back? How long before she began to depend on him and lose her ability to be a person in her own right? How much could Cord change? Could he stop being her knight and start being her man? Could he let her walk beside him, taking the same chances he did? Did he even want her that way? Love didn't always mean commitment.

Eleven

Cord stared out the window of his office. On his desk
behind him was enough work to keep him busy all day.
He had come in early just to make a dent in the pile.
He hadn't slept. He hadn't wanted to get into the bed
he and Victoria had shared. He had changed the
sheets, striving to wipe the scent of her from his
apartment. It hadn't worked. Her razor had been in
the bathroom. He had thrown it out, and the empty
place on the vanity had been a silent accusation. He
could still remember the look on her face as she had
told him to leave. Her desperation made him feel
guilty, and though he hated the feeling, he couldn't
fight it. He had hurt her, perhaps too much for her to
ever forgive him. So he sat there, listening to the
sounds of her heels as she walked down the hall to her
office. Maybelle was with her. He couldn't hear what

they were saying, but it didn't take much imagining to figure out he was the subject of the conversation.

A few minutes later he heard the door slam. Heavier footsteps than Victoria's. Maybelle. One brow lifted as he turned to face his own door. Should he see Victoria? Maybe it would be better to get it over with. They worked in the same office and he couldn't spend his time holed up in here. Rising, he took one step then changed his mind. What could he say that hadn't already been said? Angry, frustrated, he sat down again. Maybe tomorrow would be easier on both of them.

The phone rang. He reached for it, needing something to do. It was James.

"I just had an interesting visitor," he said, without bothering with a greeting. "Do you have a brother?"

Cord tensed. How could he have forgotten about Robert? Only Victoria could have driven the memory from his mind. Only she had the power.

"I do. Why?"

The silence was telling. Cord felt the anger stir. He knew what was coming. Robert was desperate.

"He came to me with the slickest scheme I've heard in years. He tried trading on your name and I told him to get lost. I felt like smashing his jaw. I thought he was lying."

"He wasn't."

"Too bad we can't pick our relatives like we pick our friends," James observed bluntly. "Save a lot of trouble in the end. What do you want to do about this?"

Cord leaned back in his chair. The first hurdle hadn't been much at all. "You aren't asking questions. Why?"

"Don't need to. Never trusted smooth-tongued people. The man's a con artist. He could sell ice cubes to Eskimos. Give me razor-blunt honesty every time."

"Thanks." Victoria had seen more than he had. She had believed in his friends. He felt guilty he hadn't had as much faith.

"For what?"

"Not getting taken in."

"Don't mention it. I'm too wily a bird for easy pluckin'." He paused, then probed carefully. "Sounds like this has happened before?"

It was getting easier to talk about Robert. Maybe Victoria had been right about that, too. Maybe he shouldn't have tried so hard to keep his existence a secret. Every family had a skeleton or two. "Too often."

"That's tough."

For the first time in his life he took a chance on a friend. "If Robert approached you, he had to be talking big bucks. If he couldn't get the money from you, he won't stop there."

"I didn't think so either. I can pass the word down the line. It won't take much to close this town to him."

"I didn't want to ask."

"Hell, man, why not? I would have asked you if the positions had been reversed," James returned bluntly. "Can't have a man like him running loose when he's so easy to stop. Of course, you know there will be talk."

"There always is."

"Does Victoria know? A thing like this could get nasty before it gets better, and she could get caught in the fallout. There are a lot of people who would like to see you take a tumble from that pedestal you're on.''

"I know. I took care of Victoria." He stretched the truth a little to protect her. "We aren't a pair anymore. The worst anyone will be able to say is that she dumped me when she found out about Robert, but she'll be out of it.''

James whistled softly. "And she agreed to this. I wouldn't have thought so, my friend."

Cord scowled, not liking the disbelief and not about to explain. "It's done. That's all that matters." The irritation was sharp in his voice. Silence.

James spoke, nothing in his tone to indicate an opinion. "I'll see that the right people get wind of what Robert's up to."

"The police are looking for him, so with any luck they'll get him before he can cause any real trouble." Cord hung up, thinking about the coming weeks. He hated gossip. People talking about things of which they knew nothing. It was so damaging, especially if one didn't have a thick hide. Victoria didn't. He did. Necessity had taught him how to publicly pretend he knew and felt nothing.

This time he intended to do nothing as well. If anyone was fool enough to be taken in after being warned, then it would have to be on their heads. He had done his last picking up after Robert. He was weary of paying another man's price.

Victoria sighed, glancing at the clock. She hadn't stirred out of her office since she had arrived. The day was proceeding normally by all appearances. Only she knew better. Her stomach was in knots as she waited for the first sight of Cord. But his door was as closed as hers. The phone rang. She picked it up, wondering at the number of calls she had received this morning. Two of them, from wives of previous clients, had been decidedly odd.

"Mrs. Maitland. What can I do for you?"

Victoria grimaced at her own voice, the sugary politeness was not her style, but it was Cora Maitland's. The woman was a society busybody, with her verbal machete always aloft, looking for a target. When Victoria had first met the woman, she had proceeded to question her ever so delicately about her own relationship with Cord, the implication being that she had earned her place in the firm by less than conventional means. Cord had been livid when he had found out, threatening to refuse to design the new Maitland home. She had barely talked him out of it.

"I just wanted to tell you how much I am enjoying my garden. You are an artist, my dear. Truly an artist."

Victoria knew that tone. The knife was out but Victoria couldn't figure out why. "I'm glad you like it," she replied, wishing the woman would drop her bomb.

"The magnolia trees are beautiful in the spring. I do so love magnolias. My sister was saying just the other day how she wishes she had a garden like mine."

"I hadn't realized that you had a sister," Victoria murmured, thinking fast and coming up empty.

"Not many people do, dear. We don't always get along. So few families do nowadays. I mean, take your partner. Look at him and his brother. Such a difference."

Victoria froze, her fingers tightening on the receiver. Shock widened her eyes. Robert? Where had Cora Maitland heard of or met Robert?

"I don't know what you mean." She played for time.

Cora's disbelieving laughter trilled in the phone. "Of course you do, dear. With you and Cord being so close. How could you not know he has a criminal for a brother? My Harold checked, bless his heart. Such a pity, too. A man like Cord Darcourte. Think of all the influential people he knows, and we are so vulnerable. After all, we have so much. It's quite difficult sometimes not to be taken in when one appeals to our humanity."

The hypocrite. As far as Victoria knew Cora Maitland was the next-best thing to Scrooge. "I really don't know what you're talking about, and I have a great deal of work to do." She hung up the phone with Cora still sputtering in the background.

How had Cora found out? She didn't, for one minute, buy that bit about Harold checking Robert out. Worry about Cord drove all thoughts of her own feelings out the window. He didn't deserve this. His door was still closed. She hesitated, then knocked. She didn't want to tell him, but better from her than someone else.

Cord recognized the knock. He leaned back and worked at looking casual. "Come in."

His eyes ran over her as she stood on the threshold, hovering, seemingly not sure whether to stay or go. He wondered what had driven her to seek him out. The faint stain of color on her cheeks told of her discomfort, yet she still came.

Victoria wanted him to look as bruised as she felt. Instead, he was the same. His expression was faintly inquiring, much as it had been each time she had come to discuss a business problem with him. Was she so easy to dismiss? she wondered as she made her feet move toward him. Maybe she was a fool to try to warn him of the gossip circulating already. Cord didn't need her or anyone. He wouldn't let himself need.

"Something wrong?" he asked, when it became apparent she wasn't going to speak. He didn't want her in his office for any longer than was necessary. He needed space and time away from her, time to stop wanting her and space to cease remembering how it had been.

"I'm not sure," she said, wishing she could be calm. "I just got a call from Cora Maitland."

Cord's brows rose at the name, recalling the hatchet-faced woman whose main enjoyment in life seemed to be listening at keyholes and peeping into closets. "So?"

There was no easy way to tell him. "She was trying to find out the situation between you and Robert."

Cord tensed, then forced himself to relax. It was what he had expected, after all. "Robert works fast. I have to give him credit for that if nothing else."

Victoria sat down, not realizing she had done so. "You mean you were expecting this?"

"It was a logical assumption given Robert's nasty streak. He wants money. He wouldn't take my refusing without retaliation. What better way than to put the bite on people I know and do business with? He already tried with James."

"But he only got to town yesterday."

Cord smiled grimly at the naïve statement. How many times had someone underestimated Robert? Too many to count. "How do you think he knew about you? Where you lived? What you were to me? I bet he has a file on anyone who has been in contact with me for the last ten years. He probably knows my bank balance and my underwear size, too. Where I buy my groceries and who I took to dinner six months ago."

"How can you stand it?" she burst out, angry at the invasion of her own privacy as well as Cord's.

"What choice do I have?" He shrugged, surprised to find he wasn't as furious as he used to be.

Victoria sat still, feeling she would shatter from the pain of the indifference in his voice. "First you deny you want me, now you act as though I don't even have the right to care about you as a friend. What do you want from me?" Her eyes were bright with unshed tears.

Cord made himself stay in his chair. Every instinct demanded that he take her in his arms, whisper all the secrets in his heart, heal them both with passion. His hands clenched on the chair arms. "I don't want anything, Tori. We're friends, but you don't have to worry over me like a mother hen with one chick. I can survive Robert and anything he can do. I have before." The control he exerted made his voice harsher than he intended. The effect was immediate.

Victoria drew back. For one moment their eyes met. She was the first to turn away. "I guess I was more of a fool than I knew," she murmured awkwardly, getting to her feet. "I—" Her voice broke. She firmed it and continued. "I have an appointment out of the office that isn't on the calendar. I won't be back for the rest of the day.'' Walking away from him was only possible by concentrating on each step.

Cord watched her go. He had thought last night was the farthest into a pit of agony he could fall. He knew better now. He loved her, and yet he would always want to keep her safe. She didn't want that. He could understand her needs, but he didn't know how to stop wanting only the best for her. He wanted her happy, and for that she needed a home and the family she always wanted. He wanted to marry her, but he was afraid to say that out loud even though he knew it was the truth. If Robert died tomorrow, his presence would still have an impact. He was no longer a well-kept secret. Cora Maitland would see to that. Victoria would know the sting of gossip, the whispers that died when she entered a room. Eventually, the gossip would fade but not necessarily the damage.

Victoria walked down the hall, too hurt to cry, to fight, to think. In all their years, Cord had never sent her away. She didn't remember going to her office and collecting her briefcase. It was only when Maybelle caught her arm, stopping her on her way out the door, that she really focused on anything but her pain.

"Victoria, what's wrong?" she demanded, looking at her worriedly.

"He called me Tori," she murmured distractedly. "He hates that name."

"He didn't mean it. I know he didn't. He's upset with this mess with Robert. You know he's not himself." Maybelle pulled on Victoria's arm, trying to lead her to the chair beside her desk. "Sit down. Tell me what happened. Maybe I can help."

Victoria shook off her hold. "No one can help. I need to get away, think. I can't do it here."

Alarmed at the deadness of her voice, Maybelle reached for her again. "Victoria, don't. One of you has to be willing to give. Cord can't. Not right now. Not with this mess hanging over him. How can he come to you? You know his pride."

"Yes, I know his and mine. But the knowing doesn't change anything." Victoria walked to the door. This time Maybelle didn't try to stop her. "I won't be back for the rest of the day. He knows, not that I think it matters."

Maybelle stood staring after Victoria. She couldn't believe Cord would let Victoria leave like this. It just wasn't in him. She glanced down the hall, biting her lip as she tried to decide what to do. She couldn't bear to see them hurting each other. Squaring her shoulders, she made up her mind. The worst he could do was fire her.

"I want to talk to you," Maybelle said when she entered his office.

Cord sighed as he looked up. Lifting a hand to his neck, he massaged the tense muscles. "If it's about Victoria, don't bother," he muttered.

"Don't tell me what to bother about. You may pay my salary, but that doesn't give you the right to tell me to stop worrying about my friends. What is it with you two? Why did Victoria go out of here looking as if she had been run over by a truck? What did you do to her?"

"You're being overly dramatic. We broke up if you must know."

Maybelle glared. "I know that. She told me. I told her she wasn't being fair. Now I think I was wrong. What is it with you? What does the woman have to do to prove she loves you?"

Emotion stirred under the layers of fatigue, guilt and defeat. "It's none of your business."

"I'm making it my business. Fire me if you want, but I will have my say." She glared at him.

"All right. Get it over with."

"Didn't you hear me? Victoria left."

"She had work to do."

"Is that all you're going to say? Aren't you worried? Aren't you going after her?"

"Yes, not especially, and no, in that order. She's a grown woman. She doesn't want a caretaker anymore." He picked up his pen. "Are you done?"

Maybelle threw up her hands and stalked out. There was no talking to Cord when he was in this kind of mood.

Cord sat still, thinking about what Maybelle had said. He hadn't liked the word pictures she had drawn. Maybelle was being overly dramatic. Victoria was not the kind of woman to behave that way. He frowned, remembering one other time when he had known her to really retreat. He rose and went to the window. He could see the parking lot from there. Her car was gone. Going back to his desk, he tried to work and couldn't. His concentration was shot. The clock in front of him counted the hours without marking Victoria's return. He buzzed Maybelle.

"Has she called in?"

"No."

He winced at the hostile reply. He was too busy running their last conversation over in his mind. He could have handled the situation better. He had been so blinded by his own needs, his wish to keep her out of Robert's way, that he had left her with nothing.

"Mr. Southerland just walked in. Shall I send him back?"

Cord was in no mood for work or talking to James. "Can he come back later? I need to go out."

"No, I can't come back later," James answered from the doorway. "You're not the only one with commitments and a business to run. This can't wait."

Cord glared irritably as he flicked off the intercom. "Then make it short," he snapped.

James took a seat, in no better mood than Cord. "All right. I want you to put double shifts on my house as soon as possible. I've got plans, and I need that thing finished to implement them."

"You could have phoned that in." Cord jotted a note to himself.

"I could have, but I didn't. I mean this, Cord. I don't care how much money it takes or what strings you have to pull—"

Cord's eyes narrowed at the tone. "Reason."

"I want to get married."

As bombs went, this was a shocker. Cord straightened in his chair, momentarily diverted from his own problems. "You? Who to? I didn't know you were dating anyone."

"I'm not."

"Sounds difficult to pull off a marriage."

"It might be impossible, but I'm going to give it a shot. And actually, you and Victoria are to blame for that."

"How?"

"I want what you two had. I intend to get it if I have to take on an army of problems to do it." He shrugged, grinning. "I never knew I had such a stubborn streak, or maybe it's pure arrogance."

"What about the woman? She might not want you. You might not be good for her or her for you."

James got to his feet. "That's the difference between us. I don't care whether we're supposed to be good for each other or not. As long as I love her and she loves me, that's all I care about. I'd be a fool to consider anything else as important."

James's words hit home in a way Cord couldn't ignore. "If there is any fool in this room, it's me." Cord rose, suddenly filled with energy. "Go away. I'll take care of getting your house done, but right now I've got more important things to do. I've just made the biggest mistake of my life. I've got to fix it." He stalked out of the room, leaving James to follow as he chose.

"I'm going after her," he tossed at Maybelle as he passed. He hardly noticed Maybelle's grin or James's amusement. "She should have known I wasn't playing with a full deck last night or today. She knows what a stubborn mule I can be. Crazy woman. Wait until I get my hands on her."

Twelve

Victoria entered her apartment. Without allowing herself to think, she stripped off her work clothes and took a shower. There was little comfort in the well-established routine or the old, favorite clothes she put on. A cup of tea helped warm her, but nothing could take the sting out of Cord's words or the way he had acted. She paced restlessly, unable to sit or lie down. Memories of the times they had spent together gave her no rest. Grabbing her keys, she left. Hardly aware of what she was doing, she drove north. The miles mounted. The city gave way to the country. She had made no conscious decision of her destination and was surprised when she found herself at the bayou, parked in front of Cord's house. Of all the places she could have come, this was the least expected. The house where it all started. Cord's retreat. The time they had spent here held some of her best memories.

Was she foolishly trying to recapture the past? The tears that had been threatening flowed in slow streams down her cheeks. She got out, drawn against her will to enter the house. Cord had given her a key the night he had asked her to live with him. The house was quiet as she entered, almost as if it were waiting for her. Her footsteps echoed on the stairs as she climbed to the second floor. The master suite looked out over the bayou. The view was spectacular, but she didn't notice. Her eyes were on the bed that they had shared. The sobs started then. The tears rained down, liquid grief that dampened her shirt. Her legs buckled and she sank onto the bed, burying her face in his pillow. It hurt to breathe, to think, and more than that, it hurt to love him.

Cord glared at the empty apartment. Where was she? She should have gone to ground here, in her home. Instead she was heaven knew where. He slammed the door and headed for his car. He would try some of her favorite spots. Victoria had to be in one of them. But he soon found that she wasn't. Angry, worried, frustrated, he scowled at the setting sun. He tried her apartment again. Swearing when he found it empty, he returned to his place.

"Where is she?" Cord stalked the empty rooms, picking up the things of Victoria's that had found their way to his home. Her brush on his dresser. The shoes she couldn't find that had gotten kicked under the sofa. The more traces of her he found, the more he paced. The last straw was the Nile-green blouse he had bought her. He held it in his hands and remembered the night he had given it to her. He had helped her fasten the tiny buttons that marched down the front, and later she had helped him unfasten them when his hands had been shaking so much with desire that he hadn't been able to remove the silk without tearing it.

Her laugh echoed in his memory. The way she had melted around him when he had entered her tightened his body with passion even now.

"Damn!" He threw the blouse across the room. It hit the wall and slithered to the floor. "The house." The idea struck from nowhere. He tensed. Would she go there? It was the only place he hadn't checked. He was in the car before he realized it.

Victoria sat staring at the fire. She should be on her way back to town, but she was too drained to make herself move. It was Friday and Cord would be arriving soon. She was a fool for coming here to a place she didn't belong and a fool for staying. She had no right in his home now. Watching the flames, she waited, unable to summon the energy to leave. The sound of a car coming up the lane made her tense. A door slammed. Cord. She couldn't move. The door to the house closed, and then he was there. Still she didn't look at him.

"Why here?" Cord asked quietly.

He watched her, waiting for her to show some sign that she knew he was there. She looked so sad, so quiet, as though she had been carved out of soft white

stone, polished with loving hands, gilded gold by the
fire before which she sat.

"It began here. It should end here."

He frowned at the emptiness in her voice. He had
driven out, vacillating between anger and need. She
had torn him up inside before, but now she was killing him. He had done this to her. He couldn't forgive
himself for his words or the way he had pushed her
away.

"Look at me," he commanded, coming a step
closer.

"What's the point? I'll just see things I'd rather not
know. Your keys are on the table. All but the apartment key. I'll leave that after I pick up my things."

Five steps brought him to her side. He caught her
shoulders and pulled her to her feet. He had come too
far. He wouldn't let her end it. If he had to start over,
he would recapture what his holding on to the past had
destroyed.

"You aren't going anywhere. Not now. Not ever."

Still she didn't look at him. All he could see was the
top of her head. He had to see her face. He had to
know what she thought, what she felt. He wouldn't let
her hide. There had been enough of that from both of
them.

"Look at me, damn it."

Victoria heard the words, wanted to reject them but
just couldn't find the energy. Somewhere between
having him throw her declaration of love back in her
face and the tears that she had poured out in his bed,
she had just stopped feeling. Nothing really mattered
anymore.

"Victoria!" He shook her once. "Fight me! Shout! Call me seven kinds of a fool! I deserve it all. But don't shut me out." He gathered her in his arms. "Damn it, you know my temper. It never used to drive you away. I didn't mean for you to run. I needed time. I felt dirty and guilty as sin for what Robert was doing and what I had to do to stop him. It isn't rational. I know that now. But I was reacting out of the past. I don't want to see you hurt, as those I have cared about have been, through him. I thought he would always be a threat to our life. I didn't want you to live with the gossip and the whispers. I knew the price you would pay for loving me."

He tilted her head up, taking her lips, warming them with his own. She was so quiet, so unresponsive in his arms. Her fire was quenched. The passion, ashes in his hands. He raised his head and glared at her.

"But I can't go through with it. I'm not as unselfish as I thought. I want you. I love you more than I have ever loved anyone in my life. And I was wrong. Very wrong. Love means giving and taking. I listened to you even if I didn't want to hear what you were saying. I know I would have been hurt if you had shut me out when you needed me after George. I devalued you as a woman and the woman I love when I tried to protect you from Robert. I know that now. I learned a tough lesson. You want to help me fight dragons, then all right."

He touched her lips gently, asking for a response. "I want you at my side in every battle. I won't promise to change completely. I wish I could. I'll try to keep you safe, but I won't ever shut you out again. Can you live with that? Can you have my children? Build a life with me?''

Victoria stared at him. The firelight bronzed his skin and carved harsh lines in his face. He was all primitive male, fighting for survival. He was saying the words she had prayed to hear. His voice was tortured, deeper, oddly more angry than she had ever heard it. But sweet. How sweet, rich and full.

"I can do anything as long as you hold me. I'd tackle a hundred Roberts for you," she whispered. "My love is tearing me apart without you in my world."

"Then marry me. Marry me and share my past, present and future. Protect me from loneliness for the rest of my days as I'll protect you. And if we fail, hold me as I'll hold you." He pulled her close, his gaze holding hers.

The tears gathered in her eyes. His face blurred. "I love you."

"Does that mean yes?" He couldn't let himself believe in the future until he heard her say the word.

"It means yes." She slipped her arms around his shoulders, holding him as tightly as he held her. "I've never been able to say no to you."

Cord lifted her in his arms, pausing only to look into her eyes. "I need you."

She clung to him. "No more than I need you. Make me your woman."

He smiled. "With pleasure. But the bed is too far away."

"The couch will do." She kissed the smile from his lips as he lowered her to the cushions.

"I wasn't sure you would listen," he admitted huskily as he unbuttoned her blouse.

Victoria returned the favor. "I wasn't sure you would talk to me."

Their jeans landed in twin piles of denim on the floor.

"I may end up talking so much that you'll buy earplugs," he murmured, trailing warm kisses over her breasts. They swelled against his mouth, silently demanding more.

"I have better ways to shut you up," she whispered, doing her own brand of sensual exploring. His breath emerged in a gasp at her adventurous advances. "You like that, do you?" She lifted her head to watch his face. Now that she knew he loved her and understood her need to be at his side in all things, she was free to look her fill, to touch him in all the ways she had been afraid would betray her secret. The knowledge was potent, demanding and exciting.

"I didn't teach you that," he muttered, his body quivering with need. "What have you been doing, sitting here thinking of ways to drive me out of my mind?"

"Thinking of ways to chain you to my side," she whispered, the teasing words not hiding the truth from either of them. Her fingers stroked slowly down his side. "I flipped between wanting your head on a platter and your body right where I have it now."

"Witch!" Cord rolled her onto her back and caught her hands. "I'm a fool."

"I know. But I love you anyway."

He stretched her arms above her head. He laughed. With her in his arms, everything was possible. "Blast you, woman. You're not supposed to agree with me." He nudged her until she adjusted to receive him.

Victoria smiled, delighting in his strengths and his power. He held her with gentleness as he mastered her body. He melted against her even as he joined them as one. They matched equally but differently.

"I call them as I see them." She raised her hips, urging him deeper. The lovely tension tightening every muscle demanded release. She denied them both, wanting to play, to stretch the joining, to savor the last drop of desire.

Cord gave her all she asked, then more. She was his—his fantasy and his reality. The years of patience and friendship were over and only just beginning. "When will you marry me?" he breathed hoarsely. He had to know she was his in all the ways there were.

"A man will say anything in the throes of passion," she returned, gasping with the words. The easy way was not for them. They had passed the point of no return. Soon. "I'll marry you as soon as I get a real proposal," she managed just as she reached the peak. "Cord!"

He caught his name as his lips covered hers. He thrust deep, spilling the essence of his power into the source of his strength. His woman. His love.

"What do you mean you want a real proposal?" he demanded when he could breathe regularly again.

Victoria raised her head from his shoulder to grin at him. Her hair was a tangled black cloud about her face. The firelight painted her limbs with red-gold shadows. She had never looked more beautiful or more desirable to Cord. He stroked her curls back from her face, watching her eyes, loving the look and feel of her.

"I mean that I want a down-on-your-knees-will-you-marry-me proposal. I've changed my mind. I'm not saying yes until I get it."

Cord's hands stilled, his eyes widening on the realization that she meant every word. As soft as she was in his arms, he had forgotten the steel in her backbone. "You're nuts. I'm too old for that kind of nonsense."

The smile slipped to a glare. "You're trying to slide out of it with that lame excuse." She pushed at his chest. She wanted all the ties. She wanted to be able to look back when she was old and gray and remember every moment, every look.

He gathered her closer. If she had asked him, he would have gotten down on his knees. But an ultimatum was too much. He had his pride, he decided with a grin. He also had an advantage. "Victoria, be reasonable. It's not even dignified."

She made a noise that in anyone else would have been called a snort. "Since when have you worried about your dignity? If you love me, you'll get on your knees. I'm forgoing a courtship you know."

"Courtship!" Cord sat up with a jerk, nearly falling off the narrow couch in the process. "What the devil do you call what we've been doing all this time? Besides, people don't court nowadays."

"They also don't fight with the woman they've just made passionate love to."

"You started it."

"I didn't. I made a perfectly reasonable suggestion."

"Order."

"Request."

He glared at her. She returned the look full measure.

Impasse.

"Do you want to negotiate?"

Victoria considered that. "What are you offering?"

He thought a minute. "Leave out the knees part."

"But that's the part I like best."

"You're pushing me, woman."

"How far?"

Cord stood up in one swift move and tossed Victoria over his shoulder. She hung upside down, smiling. "Caveman tactics don't work. This still isn't a proposal."

"It will be. I am taking you to bed. And I promise you in the morning I will have asked you again and you will have said yes. And without the knees." He stalked up the stairs, grinning. "On top of that, you're going to give up arguing with me for the sheer fun of driving me nuts. We are going to settle down and raise babies and build the best business this side of the Mississippi. By the time we do all that, neither one of us will be nipping at each other."

"Wanna bet?"

* * *

Victoria turned her head to watch Cord as he drove. She smiled a little to herself on seeing his relaxed expression. Cord was mellowing. Robert had gone out of their lives as quickly as he had come, locked away in prison with little hope of immediate release. The gossip had been uncomfortable for a while, but the people who had really mattered had simply accepted the existence of a blot on the Darcourte family tree and then forgotten it. She had hurt for Cord during that time, but she hadn't once regretted taking on his past as her own. As for Cord? Five months of marriage and a baby on the way hadn't turned him into a tame cat, but he did have moments when she could swear he purred. She grinned at the image.

Cord glanced at her. "What's that look for? You've been acting strangely for days now. What's up?" he demanded suspiciously. He had thought he had known Victoria until he had slipped the ring onto her finger. Something about the ceremony of making her his before God and man had changed her. She never missed an opportunity to tease him, to drive him wild with that mysterious look he would swear she practiced in front of the mirror every morning. She was wearing that look now.

Victoria laughed softly and scooted over to sit beside him. He wrapped an arm around her so that his hand rested just under her left breast, his fingers splayed over the small swelling of her stomach. "I'm glad we're in James's driveway so I can get rid of that seat belt," she whispered as she nipped at his ear.

Cord chuckled. "Stop teasing you little witch. You know I can't pull over here. And as for James's driveway, the thing is a quarter of a mile long and you should be wearing your belt. Anything could dart out of these woods in front of us. You and that baby are my life."

"You'd keep me safe," she murmured with complete assurance.

Her trust in him always touched him to his soul. "That does it." Cord edged the car carefully off the road and parked. "You want to play games, woman. Then I'm your man." He bent his head to capture her lips. No matter how many times he touched her, it was always as though it were the first.

Victoria gave herself up to his kiss, melting into his strength. Five months hadn't taken the edge off her desire for him. With every moment they spent together she still wanted more. And it was the same for Cord, she knew. Where some couples might have had trouble working and living together, they thrived on the close contact.

"We're going to be late," she murmured when he lifted his head.

"Do you care?"

"No, but James might."

"No, he won't, and even if he did, it serves him right for sticking me with this last-minute invitation. If he hadn't made it sound so urgent, I would be at home in bed with you right this minute."

Victoria traced the line of his lips with her fingertips, smiling as she felt his body tighten in response. "There will be time enough for that later," she promised, remembering the secret she carried. "I had other plans for tonight, too."

Cord's eyes gleamed in the full moonlight that spilled over the landscape. "You did? I like the sound of that." He glared at the house that stood on the hill a few yards farther down the road. "Whatever James wants better be important. First, we bust our tails to get this house of his ready. Made me miss my honeymoon, too. Now he's cutting into what free time we do have. There are limits to friendship."

"No, there aren't. Not with you." She hugged him, loving him in his temper. The surly bear hid a disposition of a marshmallow with the people he cared about. "You've been just as concerned about James as I have."

Cord gave her a look that said he wanted to deny the charge. "A little," he allowed, before tucking her back against his side and starting the car.

Victoria snuggled close. Soon she would tell him. It was surprising she had been able to resist spilling the beans for this long. Maybelle had already guessed, though Victoria hadn't confirmed her suspicions. She had been trying to tell Cord now for three days, but every time she thought she had the stage set something came up. And she wasn't about to blurt her news out, especially not now. Not after the decisions they had made. In all their planning for a family, they hadn't even considered this possibility.

"There's that look again." Cord parked in front of the house he had designed, ignoring it for the more fascinating subject of his wife's face. "What are you plotting?"

"How do you feel about twins?" Victoria commented vaguely.

"Twin what?" Cord replied, then stopped, a sudden thought striking. "Twins as in babies?"

She nodded. Maybe she didn't need a special setting, after all. "Would you mind?"

Cord swallowed. He had just gotten accustomed to her being pregnant. "As in the future or right now?" He eyed her slender length. He had thought she was showing a bit too much, but what did he really know about pregnancy? The books hadn't been that specific.

"Are you sure? What are we going to do? Two babies!" He leaned back, staring at her in a daze.

Victoria patted his hands, stifling her amusement. Cord looked as if he had been hit in the face with a bag of ice cubes. "We'll manage. I promise. Now you'll have a baby to handle all your own."

Cord gaped at her. "Who, me?" He laid his head against her shoulder, suddenly realizing the full import of her news. "What about your job? You're just getting established. Are you sorry? One baby would have been tough to juggle and keep your career on track. This isn't going to be a picnic."

"I know. I thought of that. But between us we can do it. I have it figured out. You take one of them in with you, and I'll take the other."

Cord stared at her. "In with me?" he asked, a sinking feeling telling him he understood more than he wanted to.

She had been no less shocked than he at the announcement of twins in her future. Starting a family at their age wasn't easy. "We talked about this. You said Darcourte was our business, and that if I wanted to bring the baby to work at first, I could. Well, we'll just do it with two. No problem.''

"No problem!'' Cord all but roared. "You were only bringing him or her to work while you were breast-feeding. *I cannot breast-feed.* The books didn't prepare me for this! I'm all for being with you in the delivery room. I don't even mind strawberry ice cream and pickles. But two babies nursing at the office?''

Victoria pulled away to watch him. He sounded honestly horrified. "I thought you wanted babies.''

"I do. But I had one at a time in mind. Twins? Trust us to hit a doubleheader the first time out,'' he muttered, his mind boggling at his vision of the future. Double cribs, double orders of diapers, double strollers, double— He swallowed hard, slamming the brakes on his thoughts. The grin started then. Double love. His and Victoria's had created two children.

Tears filled Victoria's eyes. She had counted on Cord to help her. "Do you mind?'' she whispered.

He stared at her as if she had taken leave of her senses. "You crazy woman. Why would I mind the woman I love giving me two children instead of one? You're a miracle lady.'' He hauled her into his arms, kissing the tears from her cheeks. "I love you. I don't know much about this baby stuff, but I'm willing to learn. And as long as you're happy, we'll muddle through. Haven't you caught on yet? Between us we can handle anything. Even breast-feeding twins in the middle of our office. Maybelle is going to either be in heaven or threatening to quit.''

Cord grinned with delight at the prospect of his impending dual fatherhood. "I can't wait for the next four months to be over. Just think, we're going to be parents of twins! I told you we're dynamite in bed."

Victoria laughed softly, her tears drying. She should have known Cord would never let her down. "I love an I-told-you-so man."

Friend, lover, husband, father of her children. Cord was everything to her and everything for her. He was right. Together they could do anything.

* * * * *

Watch for James and Suzanne's story,
WOMAN IN THE SHADOWS
(Desire #485), in March 1989!

"Barbara Delinsky has a butterfly's touch for nuance that brings an exquisite sheen to her work."
—*Romantic Times*

A nightmare begins for a young woman when she testifies in an arson trial. Fearing for her life, she assumes a new identity...only to risk it all for love and passion after meeting a handsome lawyer.

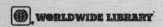

ATTRACTIVE, SPACE SAVING BOOK RACK

Display your most prized novels on this handsome and sturdy book rack. The hand-rubbed walnut finish will blend into your library decor with quiet elegance, providing a practical organizer for your favorite hard-or soft-covered books.

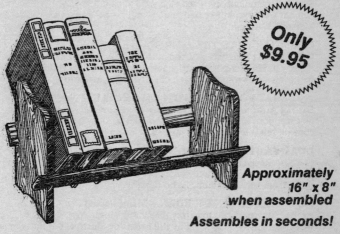

Only $9.95

Approximately 16" x 8" when assembled

Assembles in seconds!

To order, rush your name, address and zip code, along with a check or money order for $10.70* ($9.95 plus 75¢ postage and handling) payable to *Silhouette Books.*

Silhouette Books
Book Rack Offer
901 Fuhrmann Blvd.
P.O. Box 1396
Buffalo, NY 14269-1396

Offer not available in Canada.

BKR-2A

*New York and Iowa residents add appropriate sales tax.

Silhouette Desire

COMING NEXT MONTH

#469 RELUCTANT FATHER—Diana Palmer
Meet our JANUARY MAN-OF-THE-MONTH, Blake Donavan.
Tough. Formidable. He lived alone and liked it that way. His
nemesis was love, but he had one obsession—her name was
Meredith Calhoun.

#470 MONTANA'S TREASURES—Janet Bieber
G.T. Maddox loved his land too much to let Amanda Lukenas
destroy it. He figured he'd offer some old-fashioned hospitality
featuring his own special brand of . . . friendly persuasion.

#471 THAT FONTAINE WOMAN!—Helen R. Myers
District Attorney Adam Rhodes didn't like Fontaines and Diana was
no exception. She was the kind of woman he knew he could never
control, but one he ached to possess.

#472 HEARTLAND—Sherryl Woods
Friends. Steven Drake and Lara Danvers had once been much more
than that. Now Steven had come back and he wanted Lara *and* her
farm. Could she trust him . . . this time?

#473 TWILIGHT OVER EDEN—Nicole Monet
Amber Stevenson had to betray the man she loved to protect him
from scandal and disgrace. She still loved Joe Morrow, but the secrets
remained along with her passion.

#474 THIN ICE—Dixie Browning
Maggie Duncan had left a high-powered job and a failed marriage for
her grandfather's cabin. She'd found peace in her solitude—but that
was before Sam Canady arrived!

AVAILABLE NOW: